Magic in the Mountains

Mary Warren

To all those searching, may you find the magic inside of you, a community to support you and your own truth to guide you.

FOREWORD

Dear Readers,

I'm excited for you to read this story between Abe and Julie. It is a paranormal romance set in the 90's in a small mountain town. Julie does have a traumatic past so check the content warning please.

Enjoy!

Content Warning: Past abuse, mentions of sexual assault, attempted attack, violence, gun violence, past abortion, religious trauma, graphic sexual content.

PROLOGUE

Bridget
October 1996

Misty fog hid the mountains from view as Bridget's VW bus wound its way through the country roads to a familiar town. While she hadn't been back to Hecate's Hollow in many years, the ancient magic in these mountains was calling to her. She wasn't sure what she was here for yet, but she knew there was a reason their magic sang.

Nothing had changed in the little mountain town since her last visit. There was still a diner and a run-down motel. Main Street still had a drug store and empty storefronts. While the coal company never got its hands on these mountains, the poverty of the region still left its marks everywhere. Despite all of that, there was something almost ethereal about Hecate's Hollow. Bridget once spent many years with a family in these mountains.

The ancient magic that sang to her in the highlands of Scotland so long ago sang to her here now from these ancient mountains. And right now, it was a song of warning, of a coming storm.

After she made her way through the town, she drove deeper into the backwoods and turned down a little dirt road that would have been hidden to anyone not looking for it. She wound her way up the mountain on that gravel road to find an old friend. An old friend who might be able to help with whatever was brewing here in Hecate's Hollow.

CHAPTER ONE

Julie

The stench of cigarettes and stale beer hit Julie in the face as she opened the door to 4B. The ruckus of the previous night had warned that this room wouldn't be fun to clean. Beer bottles were everywhere, some empty, others almost gone with cigarette butts floating in the dregs. She pulled on her gloves with a satisfying snap and got to work.

She'd been staying at the D-Lux Motel for two months now. The owner, Dale, may have been a despicable human, but he was allowing her to stay rent-free in exchange for maid service. Some days it seemed she spent just as much time dodging his advances as she did actually cleaning rooms, but she didn't have anywhere else to go. Guests were infrequent and rarely so sloppy, so she was able to pick up shifts at the local diner. She'd managed to save a little money and hoped to get out of this situation soon.

She snapped open the trash bag and set to cleaning the room. After she threw away all the trash and cleaned up all the questionable substances that she'd learned to not think too hard about, she stripped the bed. With the trash was in the dumpster, she only had to deal with laundry. She made her way, as quietly as possible, through the back door of the office to start the load.

She tried to be quiet, as to not disturb Dale. Odds were he was in his office watching cable news and wouldn't hear her. Tossing in the soap, she closed the lid and started the washer. She was almost out the door when she heard it.

"Where are you off to so fast, girly?"

She froze, her mind racing, trying to think of anything she could say to get away from him.

"I need to go get cleaned up. I have a shift at the diner," she said.

"Not cutting out early, are you? We had three checkouts this morning."

"Yep, all the rooms are done."

"Why don't you come and sit with me in the office for a bit? We can talk about your advancement here. Then you wouldn't have to work at the diner," he drawled as he scratched his balls, leering at her.

"While I appreciate the offer, I like working at the diner. I've met a lot of people and made some good friends who'd miss me if I was gone." She let those last words linger, a warning that even though she'd only been in town a few months, people would notice her absence. She had clocked Dale as a predator the moment they met, but she didn't have any other options. And as much as she would love to find another place to live, it looked as though she was stuck there for a while.

"When you get off tonight, stop by my room." He was moving closer to her as he spoke.

"I'm closing tonight, so I'll just be heading to bed when I get home. Another time maybe." She hoped he would be drunk and passed out by the time she got back.

She managed to slip out the door before he was able to block her path. She walked briskly to her room and locked the door, threw the deadbolt, and set the two inside latches she'd installed herself. After she double-checked the door and was sure the curtains were drawn, she took the make-up bag from the dresser and pulled her savings from the secret pocket she'd sewn in. She knew exactly how much was there, but she counted it anyway, a reassuring ritual in a tenuous situation.

"Four hundred eighty-four," she said to no one, "a couple hundred more and I can rent an apartment."

Afterwards, she showered and got ready for her shift. What she said to Dale was true, she enjoyed working at the diner. Sure, there were disgruntled customers from time to time. Plenty of guys like Dale who thought that since she was a bigger girl down on her luck, she would be an easy mark for their advances. She had made some friends there though. For the first time in a long time, she allowed herself the hope that she might call a place home. She had spent years bouncing around just to survive and she was ready to settle down.

Pulling up to the diner, she took a deep breath. She always felt relieved walking in here.

"Hey there," called Betty. Julie was always happy when they shared a shift. She was an older woman who had worked there for decades and still had the frosty blue eyeshadow to prove it.

After the dinner rush, the diner emptied. Betty went on

break, and Julie kept busy. She was marrying the salt and pepper shakers when the door opened. A woman who looked to be in her late fifties walked in. She was short and round with wild red hair streaked with gray.

"Sit anywhere you like. I'll be right with you."

The woman smiled and gave her a nod, then took a seat in a booth near the back. There was something familiar about this woman, but Julie couldn't place it.

After the woman settled in, Julie went over with silverware and a menu.

"What can I get you to drink?" she asked.

"I'll have a cup of tea if ye don't mind, lass," she said in a Scottish brogue.

"Coming right up."

Julie went to prepare the tea while the woman looked over the menu. Something about this woman kept pulling her focus. She was certain she had never met her before; she would remember an accent like that, but there was something incredibly familiar about her.

She brought the woman her tea. "What else can I get for you today?"

"I think I'll have a bowl of oatmeal if ye don't mind. And I wouldn't say no to a piece of that cherry pie."

"Coming right up." She gave the table a little tap and smiled at the woman.

Oatmeal and a piece of pie at seven in the evening. That order seemed to match her for some reason.

She was dropping off her order when the door opened again. Abe Black walked in and looked over at the woman sitting in the booth towards the back of the diner. He was a tall man, possibly the tallest man Julie had ever seen. His shaggy brown hair sometimes fell over his eyes and his beard hid the rest of his face giving him an almost menacing look. But although he was always grumpy, Julie knew him always to be kind.

"Hi, Abe. Grab a seat. I'll be right with you."

He nodded politely to her as she returned to the counter. When she looked back, she was surprised to see him sitting with Ms. Oatmeal-and-Pie herself. How on earth did he know her?

She grabbed another menu and a set of silverware and returned to the table, "What can I get for you today, Abe?"

"I'm not staying," he replied. His eyes never left the woman.

"Okay... Is everything alright here?" she asked, suddenly wishing Betty was with her.

"Aye, of course, dear. Mr. Black and I are old friends."

She glanced from her to Abe and raised her eyebrow. They didn't appear to be old friends. But she knew as grumpy as he could be, Abe was not the sort of man to start a fight with an older woman in a diner. She looked at each of them again, gave them a smile, and headed back to the kitchen.

CHAPTER TWO

Abe

Abe had been out in his workshop working on a new order. He and his brother ran a woodworking business building and selling wooden furniture and other decorative accent pieces. After he finished sanding a bunch of wood for an old farm-style table, he was tired and ready to be done for the night. He was a creature of comfort and routine. Get up, work with his brother, go home, shower and eat dinner, rinse, and repeat. He liked his life up in the mountains and tended to stay up there as much as he could. It had everything he needed, he only ventured to town a couple times a month for supplies and a home-cooked meal at the diner.

So, when he walked up on the porch and saw a note stuck to his door, he knew this couldn't be good. He pulled the note from the door.

. . .

Hey big guy,

Something's in the wind. Meet me at the diner for dinner.

That was it, nothing else. This could only be one thing...Bridget. And Bridget meant trouble. Trouble and a great deal of nonsense seemed to follow her everywhere she went, and Abe was in no mood for it. But he also knew, if it wasn't just her matchmaking shenanigans, it could be actual trouble. So as much as he wanted to shower, make himself some dinner, and go to bed, it looked like he would be showering and heading into town to meet Bridget.

As Abe pulled his big blue truck up to the diner, he saw Bridget sitting at a table towards the back. She was a feisty old Scottish woman who had been a friend of his mother's. Those two were usually up to no good. When he saw Julie taking her order, he tried to ignore the small smile that found his face. He got out of his truck and watched. Julie had only been in town for a few months, but there was something about her. Abe didn't know her besides the handful of interactions they'd had in the diner, but he was drawn to her. She had a kind heart, but there was something about her he couldn't quite put his finger on. Abe stuck to himself for the most part, but something about her made him think he might make an exception for her.

But that was a thought for another day, right now he needed to go find out why Bridget was in town. He made his way into the diner.

"Hey Abe, sit wherever you like," Julie said to him with a smile.

"Thanks," he gave her a small nod then turned to Bridget waving him over.

Better get this over with, he thought.

"Abe, come sit!"

He made his way over to her and squeezed his body into the booth. It was a tight fit. He was a big man, closing in on 6'6 and had the body you would expect a big mountain man to have; lots of muscles from the work he did and lots of cushion to keep him warm in the long winters.

"Why are you here, Bridget?" he asked plainly.

"No time for pleasantries. I see nothing has changed," she said with a thick Scottish brogue and a smile on her face.

He just looked at her.

"Alright, have it your way," she said with a gentle shake of her head. "Have you noticed anything off lately?"

Off? Something off in Hecate's Hollow? There was always something off in Hecate's Hollow.

"You'll have to be a little more specific, Bridget."

Julie came and brought Bridget her food, oatmeal and a piece of pie. Figures.

"Can I get you anything?" Julie asked Abe with a smile. Her smile lit something inside of him like always, but it was more noticeable now than it ever had been.

"I'm not staying," he said, maybe a bit too gruffly. He watched regretfully as Julie's eyes danced apprehensively between him and Bridget. He hadn't meant to make her feel uncomfortable, but she turned and left.

"Level with me Bridget. What's going on? What brought you into town?"

"I'm not certain, but something is brewing here. There's a storm coming."

"So, you're here on a feeling?" he asked suspiciously.

"Abe, I'm telling ye, something's comin'."

"Okay, how long are you staying?"

"Still so full of welcome and charm," Bridget said goading him.

"I'm sorry, but you're the one who showed up out of the blue after all these years with a note on my door and some ominous vague news about a storm coming. Do you have a place to stay?" He would still offer her his cabin because he may be grumpy, but he was a gentleman.

"I think I'm going to stay at the motel off the interstate?"

"By choice?"

"Not entirely, but I feel like it is the right thing to do."

"Well, if anything changes my cabin is open to you."

"I appreciate that, but you really haven't noticed anything?" she asked with a discerning look.

"I haven't, I'll let you know if I do. I'm going to head home, but I'm sure I'll see you around."

"That ye will. Have a nice night, laddie," she said with a mischievous grin. She knew he hated that.

"Goodbye, Bridget."

Abe made his way out of the diner, stopping once to look back at Julie. She gave a small smile. He returned a curt nod and made his way to his truck. His trusty old blue truck rumbled to life, and he pulled out of the parking lot.

His mind kept finding its way back to Julie. His mind often found its way to her, but he couldn't figure out why. For the most part, he stayed up on his mountain, but when he did come down for supplies and a meal, seeing her had been something he found himself looking forward to.

Most of West Virginia had been mined and left without the resources that belonged to them, but this particular area had remained untouched. There was still little to no opportunity in a small town like this tucked back in the mountains, but Abe liked it just fine.

His big truck turned onto a hidden road off the highway and started to wind its way up to his cabin, but then drove past it. His brother had a cabin further up the mountain. Pulling up to it, he turned his truck off and set out to the barn that was behind the small cabin.

"Asher," he called out as he entered their workspace.

"What are you doing back here?" asked his brother as he stepped around the corner wiping some paint off his hands.

Asher was tall, not as tall as Abe, but tall, nonetheless. But where Abe was big and burly, Asher was lean and muscular with long curly brown hair pulled back in a top knot on his head.

"When I went home, I had a note on my door," he said with a heavy sigh.

"Oh yeah," said Asher. He walked over to the sink and waited for Abe to continue while he washed his hands.

"Bridget's in town."

Asher's head snapped towards him. "Bridget who?" he asked, turning off the water.

"The only Bridget we know."

"Why is she here?" Asher asked skeptically.

"I don't know. You know how she is. She said something cryptic about a coming storm," Abe said with a shake of his head.

"Weren't you just saying something felt off the other day?"

"Yeah, but I figured I was just feeling winter coming. But it looks like it might be something else."

"Is she staying at your place?"

"No, that's the other thing. She's staying at the motel."

"By choice?" Asher asked with a shocked look on his face.

"That's what I said," Abe said with a low chuckle. "I'm not sure what's going on but keep an eye out."

"Have you heard from Esther?" Asher asked with a hint of apprehension.

"No."

And that was all there was to say about that. The Black family stayed here on the mountain. They had for generations. But Esther, Abe's twin sister, had chosen to get married and left about ten years ago. Abe had begged her not to go, but in the end, it was all in vain. She left and he didn't like to talk about it.

"What do you know about Julie?" Abe asked.

Asher looked at him and cocked his head. "Julie who?"

"The new waitress down at the diner."

"The one with the juicy ass?" Asher asked with a smile on his face.

Somewhere from deep inside Abe, a growl rumbled through him. "Don't talk about her like that!"

Asher put his hands up, "I didn't mean anything, just stating a fact. She does have a nice ass. But I can see you're staking your claim."

"I am not," he grunted out.

"The way you just growled at me would say differently."

"It's not like that. I'm just worried she's caught up in all of this." Okay, so he was attracted to her, but mostly, he was concerned about her.

"Okay, I'll keep an eye out. It'll be good to see Bridget. I don't think I've seen her since I was a kid," said Asher.

"She hasn't changed one bit, still as infuriating as ever," Abe grumbled.

"Everyone's infuriating to you, man."

He hummed. "I'm going to my cabin. I just wanted to

pass along the message. I'll see you tomorrow and hopefully, we can finish up the Taylor order."

Without waiting for Asher to say goodbye, Abe made his way to his truck. He wasn't sure what was coming, but the storm he had hoped was just the coming winter may end up being more. He wasn't ready for whatever Bridget was sensing, but he would be there. He and Asher would be there to protect this mountain from whatever came its way, because that was the way of things. He just hoped they could get it all finished up before he felt the need to hibernate for the winter in his cozy warm cabin.

CHAPTER THREE

Julie

After her shift at the diner, Julie pulled up to the motel. The office lights were out. No more Dale for the night, she sighed with relief. Safely locked in her room, she sat down and counted her tips. Thirty-three dollars tonight, which wasn't bad, all things considered. She slid the bills into their secret pocket and got in the shower.

After she was all cleaned up, she took a few dollars and headed to the vending machine to make some dinner choices. While trying to straighten her dollar enough to get the persnickety old vending machine to accept it, she was surprised to see the same woman she had served earlier at the diner.

"Hello again," she said as she approached the vending machine.

The machine finally accepted her dollar. "Hello. I didn't

know you were staying here," she said, retrieving her chips when they dropped.

"Oh, I'm only passing through. I'll be here for a couple of days, then I'll be on my way."

"Your accent. Are you from Scotland?" Julie asked.

"Aye."

"Wow, that's so cool. I have never met anyone from a different country before."

"Well, I'm Bridget, pleased to meet ye." She extended her hand and Julie took it and gave it a firm shake. As their hands met, Julie felt a wave of energy pass through her. She tried to shake the lingering sensation of it. While it wasn't unpleasant, it was definitely unexpected.

"I'm Julie. It's nice to meet you. I'll see you around," she said. Then turned to make her way back to her room, but not before looking back at this mysterious woman. There was something about her Julie couldn't quite wrap her head around. The woman pulled out her candy bar from the machine, and turned, and gave Julie a little wave. Hopefully, she would be able to talk to her more during her stay in Hecate's Hollow.

Later that night Julie was in bed attempting to fall asleep. She had double-checked all her locks but anxiety still crept in. She heard footsteps approach outside her door and watched as a shadow stopped on the other side. There was a soft knock. Pulling the covers up close, she hoped he would go away. She knew who it was, and his audacity was at an all-time high. He had never come to her door after midnight before.

She watched in horror as the doorknob shook. Her heart thundered in her chest. This couldn't happen. She'd tried to outrun her past, outrun men like this her whole life. She didn't want to leave again but knew she couldn't stay here.

Not after tonight, his advances were becoming more and more persistent. Gripping the bat she kept by her bed, she watched as the deadbolt turned. He was keying his way into her room and the flimsy latches she had installed for her own peace of mind would be no match for him. She flipped through all the options in her head and found nowhere else to go.

"Excuse me, sir. What exactly are ye doing creeping into a young woman's room after midnight?" asked a familiar voice.

"Mind your own business, lady," he grumbled. "The girl works for me, and we have some unfinished business."

"I don't think I will be mindin' my own business tonight, but you will," she said, voice sounding pleasant as ever. "I'm going to ask ye one more time to leave this poor lass alone. Now."

"Or what? What are you gonna do about it?" he asked, menacing her.

"This is yer last warning," she said, her voice still holding no animus.

"Get out of my way, lady." She heard him push her aside.

"Well, that was a poor decision." Her voice sounded different this time.

Suddenly there was a strike of thunder loud enough to shake the windows.

"You will leave this poor child alone. Is that quite clear?"

"Y-y-y-yes, ma'am," he sputtered out.

"Good, she'll be checking out in the morning. Now clear out of here and go clean yourself up. You seem to have wet yourself," she said with an unbothered chuckle.

Who was this woman? she thought. Whoever she was, she was grateful she was here tonight.

There was a small knock at the door. "He's gone. Can I speak with ye, love?"

Julie made herself get out of bed. She was a little shaken and weak on her feet but made her way over to the door and cracked it open.

"It's alright, lass," the woman said. "Truly, he's gone. May I come in?"

Julie opened the door and the woman slipped in, and she quickly locked the door behind them.

"You can't stay here anymore, lass. I don't think he'll stop; I could sense it in him."

"I have nowhere else to go," she pled as panic rose in her. She knew she needed to leave but was tired of moving around, always being new and invisible.

"Don't worry your sweet head, dear. I know a place you can stay."

She looked at the woman, eyes full of wonder. "Are you serious?"

"Aye, I'll meet you at the diner first thing in the morning and take ye there. He'll bother ye no more tonight. Can you pack yer things and be ready by the morning?" she asked.

"Yes, I can be ready anytime."

"Good. Tomorrow morning as soon as the diner opens." She gave Julie's hand a quick squeeze and left. Julie locked the door behind her and tried to take a deep breath. That could have been bad, really bad. Hopefully, the place this woman had in mind would work out, or else it looked like she was packing up and hitting the road again.

Julie didn't sleep the rest of the night. Her packing had only consisted of a large duffle bag and her purse. That morning, she dropped them in her car and headed into the diner as the sun was starting to rise.

Betty was flipping around the open sign when she approached. "Goodness Julie, what are you doing here so early this morning?"

"I'm meeting someone."

"Meeting someone?" Her eyebrows flew up and her mouth opened wide. "As in maybe someone you spent the night with?"

Just then Bridget pulled up in a purple retro Volkswagen van. That seemed like a fitting car for her. She got out of the van and waved to Julie.

"No, I'm meeting her."

"She might be a little old for you. She looks almost as old as me, but love is love," Betty joked.

"You're a spry young chicken compared to me," Bridget said to Betty.

Julie chuckled and followed them into the diner.

"You ladies sit anywhere ya like, I'll get you some coffee," Betty said as she turned to start the coffee brewing.

"Tea for me please," Bridget called out.

"Coming right up."

The two women sat down at the same booth she had been at yesterday. Bridget reached over and held her hand. The strange sensation pulsed through her body again.

"Are you feeling alright this morning, lass? I know last night was one helluva night."

"Yeah, I'm okay. Thank you so much for what you did," she said in earnest.

"Please, don't mention it. We have to stick together," she said with a wink.

Betty approached their table, setting down the tea and

coffee. "What can I get for you two lovely ladies this morning? Do you need a menu?"

"Oatmeal and fresh berries for me, please. And I wouldn't say no to a slice of that pie," Bridget said with a cheeky smile.

"Pie for breakfast, a woman after my own heart. What about you Julie?"

"I'm good with coffee," Julie said.

"I'm payin' lass, please eat something," she said.

"Oh... ummm. Okay, oatmeal for me too."

Bridget glanced at the waitress's name tag. "Betty, it seems our Julie is too polite to order the delicious breakfast I am *dying* to pay for. Do you happen to know what her favorite thing on the menu is?"

"French Toast with extra bacon. At least that's what she ate on her birthday," she said with a grin.

"Perfect, please bring that."

“You got it,” she said, tapping her pen on her notepad. Betty made her way back to the kitchen as some of the morning crowd started to filter in asking for their coffee.

"You really didn't have to do that," Julie said.

"Nonsense, I'm happy to buy yer breakfast, dear. We may have a bit of a challenge when we finish here, so eat up."

"A challenge?" Julie questioned. She didn't like the sound of that.

"Nothing I can't handle. So, I'm interested, how'd you come to be in this little town staying in that awful motel?"

The gears in Julie's head began turning but her mind was blank. She'd been reinventing herself for so many years, she struggled to remember the story she used here.

"I've just kind of been hopping around trying to make ends meet. Life is hard. I've been saving up for an apartment and should be able to get one in a couple more weeks. I just had to keep cleaning the rooms. That's why he let me stay there for free."

Bridget gave her a warm smile and nodded her head knowingly.

"Dodging my questions I see, but don't worry darlin' I'll not be pushin'. Ye can tell me when yer are ready," she said kindly.

Betty brought over their breakfast. Her mouth instantly watered. She hadn't eaten anything this decadent in a very long time. When she had managed to get a room with a kitchenette she would cook, but mostly it was vending machines and gas station food. After a life of scarcity, one would think her body would stop holding onto extra weight, but the wide hips and soft belly never went away.

They ate breakfast in comfortable silence, which was good because Julie wasn't sure what to say. She was glad this woman wanted to help her. Last night had rattled her, but she wouldn't allow herself to think about that here. Too many old demons lived in those thoughts.

She popped her last piece of bacon into her mouth, while Bridget finished her pie.

"Alright lass," Bridget said. "Would you like to follow me or ride with me?"

"I'd like to follow you," she said quickly. If things ended badly, at least she'd have her car.

Bridget settled the bill and they left. Julie got into her car and she followed Bridget out to the edge of town. They continued on a gravel road, climbing higher and higher up the mountain. Anxiety started bubbling up inside of her the higher they climbed. She trusted Bridget more than she had any right to but couldn't shake the apprehension of her decision as she followed a stranger up a mountain into the backwoods. The forest began to close in around them. She could swear she saw a large animal lurking in the woods, but she never got a good look.

One last bend in the road revealed a clearing in which sat a little rustic log cabin. While she wasn't even sure if this place even had running water, it definitely had a certain charm. Bridget pulled up to the house and got out. Fighting her apprehension, Julie did the same.

When she opened the door and stepped outside, everything felt different. A wave of energy similar to what she felt when she shook Bridget's hand washed over her. She didn't know how to describe it. Something about this place, a place that she had never been to, felt like home.

"Where are we?" she asked.

"This cabin belongs to an old friend. With it being hunting season, he's sure to be livin' further up the mountain in his hunting cabin."

"Further up the mountain? We're pretty high up right now."

Bridget walked to the door and knocked. They waited for a few moments and Bridget knocked again.

"He must not be home," Julie said. She felt strangely disappointed, but it was probably for the best.

"No, he's here." Bridget appeared to be looking around like her friend was just going to pop up out of nowhere.

There was a rustling to their left and Julie looked to see Abraham Black step out of the woods, looking as grumpy as ever.

"What are you doing all the way up here?" he asked as he folded his arms over his large chest.

"I was hoping Julie could stay with you for a little while, until she gets back on her feet."

"No." He turned and walked into the house and shut the door, but Bridget bustled into the house behind him.

She could hear the two of them arguing. She didn't want to stay here if she wasn't welcome, but something about this place did make her want to stay. In the end, though, it was up to him.

The front door opened, and they walked out onto the front porch. "You can stay," he said gruffly.

"I don't want to intrude." She desperately wanted to stay but wouldn't force the issue. This was his house.

"No, I'm sorry, Julie," he said with a new kindness in his voice. "I was caught by surprise. I don't get many visitors up here. Bridget explained the situation. You can stay here as long as you need to. I have a cabin a ways up the mountain. I'll stay there, but I can keep an eye on things and make sure everything is okay."

Bridget stood next to him, her hands on her hips beaming up at him. It was quite the sight. Abe stood unnaturally tall next to this woman who was probably five feet on a good day. And oddly, Julie got the feeling this little woman was the one in charge here.

"Really? I don't want to be an imposition," said Julie.

"Och, don't mind this grumpy ol' coot." Bridget gave him an elbow to the ribs, and he raised an eyebrow and looked down at her. "He may seem unhappy now, but I know he's delighted to have you here."

She heard a low growl from Abe, and he looked down at Bridget with a less than pleased expression. Bridget just patted him on the hand. "I'll let you two get settled. I'm going back to the motel. I'm interested in how that foul little bugger will receive your exit."

Looking over at Julie, Abe's expression softened, and he gave her a small smile. Well, the corner of his mouth turned up just the slightest bit, but that was as good as it got with him.

Julie got to know him a little bit in her couple months in town. He was good people, grumpy people, but good people, nonetheless. Julie had always felt oddly drawn to him, which was surprising because she tended to steer clear from all men, even the ones she thought to be safe.

Bridget gave Julie's hand a little squeeze before climbing into her van and starting it up. Her rational side seemed to be screaming that this was all wrong. Julie had survived this long and didn't do so by following strange women into the backcountry or entering the houses of men without witnesses. However, a quieter, kinder voice told her she was safe here.

"Come on in, I'm happy to have you stay here as long as you need." She looked up at his face and saw both corners of his mouth were slightly upturned. Something clicked inside, and relief washed over her like it had when she first got out of her car. It was a feeling she hadn't had in a very long time, yet she had just experienced twice this morning.

The cabin was charming and much more modern on the inside than she would have thought. There was a dining area with a decent-sized wooden table. To the left was a small kitchen, full-sized refrigerator, counters with a sink next to a stove, and an island with a wooden countertop separating the two spaces. To the right was a small sitting area with a comfortable-looking couch with a homemade blanket thrown over the back and a small, wall-mounted TV located next to a cozy fireplace. She could see steep stairs leading up to a loft and a door next to those stairs that she guessed was the bathroom.

"It's not much. The bedroom is upstairs." He seemed

nervous, which was something that Julie had never seen before.

"This is absolutely lovely! This is the best place I have seen in my whole life." She wasn't lying, this really was a little slice of heaven for her. She had grown up in a house that looked nice on the outside, but the inside was sterile and harsh. This house was cozy and warm. She couldn't imagine a better place to land while she got on her feet.

"You're serious?" he asked.

She looked around, tears pooling in her eyes. She blinked them away and looked up at Abe and nodded her head. His body stiffened. For a moment, he looked like he might reach out and comfort her, but then thought better of it. He shoved his hands into his pockets and cleared his throat.

"I'm glad it's to your liking. Like I said, I'll be staying at my hunting cabin so you're free to stay here as long as you need. Do you need to go to work tonight?"

"Yeah, I have my uniform in my bag. I work two to close tonight."

"I'll come down when you're off to help you find the way back here. The turn can be tricky to find in the dark."

"That shouldn't be necessary, I'm sure I can find it," she said, not wanting to inconvenience him further.

"I'll be there all the same," he said with a tone of finality. "I'll leave you to get settled." Giving her one last half smile, he turned to leave.

After Abe had left, she took in the cabin's interior in quiet disbelief. She hadn't caught a break in years, but this felt promising.

CHAPTER FOUR

Julie

She was finishing up her shift at the diner, and though she had told Abe that she'd be able to find the place without him, he was there. He'd arrived about forty-five minutes before her shift ended. He and Bridget were sitting down to a meal. They were in the back corner booth engaged in what appeared to be a serious discussion. Julie brought them each the evening special, chicken pot pie, and of course, a slice of peach pie for Bridget.

Julie felt Abe watching her as she finished up, but not in the leering way she was used to. She couldn't quite identify his expression, but he seemed to regard her as a mystery. Which she understood because he was a mystery to her as well.

"I'm done here for the night, if you're here for me," she said as she approached him.

"I told you I'd be here."

"You did. I have to grab my purse from the back and lock up, but I'll meet you in the parking lot in a few minutes."

She watched him walk out to his big blue truck and couldn't help but smile. She almost felt lucky, but she didn't dare admit that. Luck was something she hadn't had for a while. She flipped over the closed sign and headed into the back room to grab her purse.

When she turned the corner, she knew her luck had run out. There, in dirty jeans and a stained Marlboro t-shirt reeking of alcohol, was Dale.

"You think you can leave without even saying goodbye, girly?" he said, leering at her. She knew she was in a dangerous situation, but Abe was in the parking lot. She just had to get to Abe. She turned to run, but he managed to maneuver his way between her and the door just as she reached it, slamming her fingers in the door.

"Fuck!" she cried out, yanking her fingers from the door.

"You still have work to do at the motel. I'm taking you back."

"I found another place to stay. I cleaned the rooms while I stayed. I kept up my end of the bargain."

"There was a little more to the bargain than that, and we both know it."

"No. There wasn't."

He just looked at her. She scanned the room, looking for a way out. There was a small window she doubted she could get out of, but she knew she had to try. She made a break for the window and yanked like hell.

He was right behind her pulling her down. His hands slid under her skirt gripping her bare thighs. She spun around, flattened her back against the window and started hitting and kicking at him. She managed to land a decent left hook, causing him to stagger. His dirt-crusted fingernails came away covered in blood to reveal a face masked in blood and cold malice.

With a renewed fervor, he grabbed her arms and pinned her against the wall.

With a crash, the storeroom door burst open, and Abe was in the doorway, growling. Dale whipped his head around, and somehow found the balls to say, "This is none of your business. This girl owes me."

"Take your hands off her before I rip them from your body."

Julie got the impression he wasn’t exaggerating.

Dale seemed to pick up on that too. He released her arms. "This isn't over," he said as he took a step back.

Abe moved like he would make sure it was over, but she couldn’t let him get in trouble. "Stop, please, he's not worth it. I just want to go home," she pleaded.

"Go get in my truck and lock the door," he said, leaving no room for argument.

"Please," she begged.

"I won’t hurt him, but we need to reach an understanding."

Julie glanced back at Dale to catch fear flit across his face.

She went out and climbed into his truck. It smelled like Abe, and it had the same comforting feeling as the cabin. She almost began to relax, but she knew if she relaxed, she would fall apart. That could’ve been really bad, but she refused to go there. So, for now, she waited numbly for Abe, hoping he returned soon.

CHAPTER FIVE

Abe

Abe watched as Julie left the room. Once he heard her leave the diner his menacing gaze turned back to Dale.

"Look, Abe. I got no beef with you. I'm not sure what she told you, but she left the motel without a word, and she still has some work--"

Abe released a low growl, cutting him off.

"I mean it, Abe," Dale continued, "don't come between me and Julie. She owes me."

"She owes you nothing," Abe growled out. "She is no concern of yours now."

"Abe--" he protested, but he couldn't quite control the fear dancing behind his eyes as Abe made his way over to him. Abe's big hand landed with a thud on his chest and fisted his hands in his shirt, pressing him into the wall. Not hard enough to hurt him, but plenty hard enough to let him know Abe wasn't messing around.

"There is no need to make an enemy today. But know this, if you even think about coming after her again, it will be the last thing you do. Do you understand me?"

Dale nodded. Abe gave his chest one last shove for good measure.

"Good, now get the fuck out of here."

The two men engaged in an icy stare, but Abe wasn't backing down. The pull he felt to protect Julie was something he felt deep down in his core. He had never been a violent man, preferring to leave the fighting to his siblings, but he knew he would kill this measly excuse of a man if he ever put another hand on her.

Dale broke eye contact first and sulked out of the diner. Abe followed closely behind him, checking the diner door was locked before making his way over to his truck. His body still pulsed with anger, he tried to breathe that all away because he needed to make sure Julie was alright. He wanted to hold her and protect her. That was an urge he hadn't felt in a long time, and he had never felt it this strongly.

As he opened the door the sight of her huddled in his truck nearly broke him. He was regretting his decision to not beat the crap out of Dale, but that wouldn't have fixed the look on her face that gutted him.

"Are you okay?" he asked, his eyebrows tight with concern as he opened his door.

She nodded as he climbed in. "I'm okay, luckily you were there."

"Are you sure? Do you need medical attention? Police?"

"No. Please, I just want to go home."

"Are you sure?"

She nodded and hugged her arms around herself. His jaw clenched, but he put the key in the ignition. The anger boiled inside of him as he thought about how long she'd stayed in that motel. Had he done this before?

"Did he mess with you at the motel?" he growled under his breath.

"Never like that," she said. "He made passes at me, but that was it. He tried to come into my room last night, but Bridget stopped him."

"Never before?"

"No, never like that."

His shoulders relaxed and he took a deep breath. "He won't bother you again."

Revving the truck to life, he set off on their way home. He knew he had told her he would be there tonight, and maybe she should have driven her own car back, but right now, he wasn't letting her out of his sight. It did cool him down a little bit to know the little weasel had never tried anything like this before, but barely.

The ride home was quiet. Abe kept sneaking glances over at Julie, but she was quietly looking out the window. He couldn't get a read on her, but he got the impression this wasn't the first time something like this had happened, even if it hadn't been with Dale. He was also quite sure the storm Bridget had been talking about had something to do with Julie and Dale. There was an idea percolating in the back of his mind. There was more to this situation than met the eye, but he would need to check in with Bridget to be sure.

Abe's hands itched with the need to comfort her. He yearned to speak words that would help her to feel better, but he wasn't sure he could. He wasn't the type of person who knew what to say or who made people feel comfortable. He was quite the opposite in fact. That had never bothered him. In fact, he preferred it that way. That was until this moment because all he wanted to do right now was scoop her up and take away all her worries.

When they turned onto the gravel road that led up to his cabin, he took a deep breath. Being on his land always calmed him. He stole one final glance at Julie as they climbed the mountain to his cabin, and to his pleasure, she seemed to relax a little bit too. Her face looked up at the sky as some of the anxiety fell away. That made him feel better, if only slightly. He would feel much better when she was safe and tucked away in his cozy cabin without creeps like Dale to worry about.

CHAPTER
SIX

Julie

She stared up at the stars as they drove up the gravel road to the cabin. There was something she had always found soothing about looking up at the stars from a moving car. They always stayed still as she sped down the road. It comforted her to know that no matter how fast and out of control things got, there were always constants. They were hard to find sometimes but if she was still enough, she could always find something.

The the gravel crunched beneath the tires as they pulled up to the cabin. She was glad to be in his truck for several reasons. One clearly being she was still shaken and in no state to drive, but she likely would have missed that turn-off. It really did come out of nowhere. It felt good to be on his land and near the cabin.

He cut the engine, and everything went quiet. The two of them just sat in the truck for a moment letting the stillness of the woods and mountains at night settle them. The only sound was the chirp of crickets and the occasional hoot of an owl. The only light was from the moon and stars overhead. The tension left her shoulders as she let out an audible sigh.

Abe got out and walked over to open her door to help her down. He shut the door behind her, but his eyes never left her. He seemed to be evaluating her, making sure she was all right.

"Is there anything you need? Anything at all?"

"No," she said looking up at him. "I'm all good. I think I just want to take a shower and go to bed."

"Would you like me to stay?" His eyes held a deep level of earnestness. If she was being honest with herself, she did want him to stay. That thought scared her.

"I think I'm okay, really. I mean unless you want to stay. It's your house, so do whatever you want."

"I want you to think of this as your house while you're here. You decide who comes in. That includes me."

"Thank you." She wanted to say more, she needed to say more but she was overwhelmed. This was new territory for her. She'd never been on the receiving end of such kindness before.

"If you need me for any reason at all, just ring this and I'll be here as fast as I can," he said, showing her a big metal triangle hanging from a rope with a striker attached. She nodded. He opened the door for her but didn't step inside. "I don't always keep it locked since no one in these parts can find it, but I do want you to keep it locked when you are here by yourself. I'd feel better."

"Of course, thanks again, for everything." Her voice caught on the last word, and before she knew what was happening, she was weeping. All the pent-up fear and desperation was bubbling up. She knew once the floodgates were opened it was impossible to shut them off. It was better just to give over and lose herself to a good cry. She needed this release, she just wished she wasn't crying in front of this handsome man who had just saved her life in more ways than one.

"Can I give you a hug?" he asked.

She nodded and sniffed. Before she knew it, she was wrapped in his arms. He was so much bigger than she was, which was impressive, because she wasn't exactly small. Warmth radiated from his body into her own. Something about this felt different.

Then, all the sudden, the world fell away. It was just the two of them in a warm, comforting embrace. A warm breeze blew around them and the earth shifted under her feet. She opened her eyes which were once streaming with tears, but now they were open in amazement.

She looked up at Abe, whose arms were still wrapped securely around her, his eyes seemed to be open and taking in what was happening too.

"What is this?" she asked.

"I'm not sure, but I don't think it is anything to worry about." He was looking out into the woods on alert, but with no sense of fear, more of wonder.

She laid her head on his broad strong chest. His heart thumped and the rhythm matched her own perfectly. She tightened her hold around his waist, and he did the same, pulling her in close. He rested his chin on top of her head and breathed in. There was a satisfied rumble deep inside of him that made her wish she could cuddle in even deeper.

They stood like that for a long moment, just enjoying the nearness of each other. It was a new feeling, but a welcome one. She hadn't known how much she needed to feel this, to feel protected and safe. She knew in her bones she was safe here, both on this mountain and in his embrace.

She felt the tears coming back. Her body shook with the few sobs she was trying to hold back, and he just stood there, holding her. His hand began to stroke up and down her back, comforting her. She cried about what happened at the diner. She cried about what happened at the motel, what had happened in every motel she had stayed in over the years, the family that had kicked her out, and the boyfriend who had abandoned her. She cried because being scared and lonely all those years was hard. It all poured out of her. The way they held each other, it felt like he was taking some of that burden on himself, like he would help her shoulder some of the invisible load she had carried by herself for so long.

After a long time, she pulled away and looked up at him. He was looking down at her with almost reverence. She felt the strong urge to kiss him but pushed that thought far from her head. That was not an urge she often had nor was it one she knew how to deal with right now. All the same, she was relieved to be with him, and his big body full of muscles and softness that would keep her safe. The look in his eyes made her feel wanted, which was something she hadn't felt in a very long time.

"If you did want to come in and talk, it might be okay. Talking might be a good distraction." She made sure to say talking twice because she didn't want him to get the wrong idea. But she already knew even if he wanted something more from her, he would never force her or even make her feel uncomfortable.

"If you'd like that. I'd like to come in and keep you company for a bit."

As they entered the cabin, he switched on the light by the door. It was just as cozy as she remembered it.

"Have you eaten anything?" he asked.

"No, I'm okay though."

"Nonsense, you go take a shower, and I'll make you some dinner."

"Are you sure?" she asked.

"Of course, please, go shower. When you're done, I'll have something ready for you."

"Thank you. I don't recall the last time anyone has shown me such kindness."

The same earnestness from the porch found his eyes now and he nodded. But now that she was looking at him in the brightness of the cabin, she could more clearly see his features. His shaggy brown hair fell around deep brown eyes that were filled with kindness and concern. He was a towering presence: he had to be over 6 '6, and he was big and soft and safe, and she just wanted to crawl up into his lap and take a long nap. *Where were these thoughts coming from?*

She snapped back to the world and climbed up the steep stairs to the bedroom, retrieved a change of clothes, then headed to the shower. She looked in the mirror and realized she looked a mess. Her hair, which had previously been pulled into a nice, neat ponytail, had parts of it completely pulled out and tangled up. Her eyes were red and puffy, and mascara ran down her face. She groaned in embarrassment at looking like this in front of Abe. Then she recalled his face. He hadn't seemed to care one bit. It was too early for a girl like Julie to have hope that the tides were beginning to turn in her favor, but there were little glimmers of hope everywhere she looked.

Once she finished showering, she opened the bathroom

door and was hit by the savory smell of what Abe was cooking. She hadn't eaten since the French toast that morning which felt like ages ago.

"How are you feeling now?" he asked. Kindness and something she couldn't quite place twinkled in his eyes as he stood at the stove spooning up some fried potatoes onto a plate.

"Much better," she said.

He picked up the plate, carried it over to a place setting at the table, revealing a cheeseburger and fried potatoes. She walked to him and hovered, not sure what to do.

"Please sit down. I hope this is acceptable."

She sat and eyed the food, awestruck. After a moment she managed to speak, "This looks great. Thank you so much. You really didn't have to go to all that trouble."

She took a bite.

“I hope it’s to your liking,” he said.

"Yeah, it's good." She took a drink of water and began eating in earnest. She was trying to be polite of course, but she hadn't eaten since morning, and now that the fight or flight adrenaline was gone, she was starving. "I'm sorry," she said after she swallowed a bite of burger. "I guess I was hungrier than I thought."

He smiled at her warmly. "Please, eat your fill. There is more where that came from."

"So, what do you do? I know I’ve seen you around, but I don't know much about you,” Julie said.

"I mostly work and live off of the land. This land has been in my family for a long time."

"I mean, you’re clearly not off-grid," she said, gesturing to the electric lights above them.

"No, I’m not, but I'm about as far off as you can get. To

pay the bills, I'm a woodworker. I make small furniture, and I carve pieces."

"Did you make anything here?" she asked.

"I made almost everything here."

She looked around at the cabin, taking it all in. There were a lot of beautiful wood pieces, from furniture to decorations.

"Wow, you're really talented."

"Thank you. Can I ask what brought you to the area?"

She felt the familiar rush of panic that accompanied inquiries into her story. It wasn't something she ever told truthfully, but she was thinking maybe it was time she did.

"If you don't wish to share with me, that's all right," he said quickly.

"No, I do want to tell you. I just don't usually share my story with people."

He looked at her, again with wonder in his eyes. A small smile crept across his face, and he patiently waited for her to share whatever part of herself she felt comfortable sharing.

"I've been in town for a couple months; I'm saving up for an apartment of my own." She took a deep breath, that was what she shared with everyone, that was the easy part. "I've been a little down on my luck in recent years, bouncing around from place to place."

"Don't you have any family to help you?"

"No. My family kicked me out when I was seventeen. I've been on my own ever since. I've been robbed, I've been attacked by creeps like Dale, I've lived in my car, but in every new town I try to have hope for a new beginning. It just never seems to work out for me."

"I'm sorry you've had such a hard time. You can stay

here as long as you like. Just know you're safe and wanted here."

She looked up at him, she had no idea how much she needed to hear that she was wanted. Those were words she had never recalled hearing before. She wouldn't cry again. She refused. "Thank you, but why are you being so nice to me?" she asked. It may have come out more accusatory than she meant, but as nice as this was, she didn't really understand where it was coming from.

"Bridget is an old friend. She told me you needed help, and I've learned not to question her. She was right about this, too. I feel protective of you. So please don't worry, I'll keep you safe. While it should go without saying, I know sometimes it needs to be said. I would never harm you. Ever. It's important to me that you know that."

"I do. Thank you."

"Well, I'd better be going, but please if you need anything at all, just ring the bell."

She didn't want him to go, but she wasn't certain why. She instinctively reached for his hand as he stood up. That strange sensation that had hit them when they were on the porch came again. It was smaller this time, but it was still there, like there was magic dancing between them. She didn't know how to explain, but she knew she didn't want him to leave. But she also wasn't ready to ask him to stay.

She looked up at him. His eyes were pinned to their hands. She could tell he felt it too. His mouth parted slightly as he looked at their hands. Before he could say anything, she pulled her hand back and stood up. The chair behind her fell to the floor making a loud racket that seemed to pull them both out of the moment.

"Right." He cleared his throat. "I'm going to head out,

but if you don't mind, I'll be here in the morning. Do I need to take you to work since we left your car there?"

"No, I'm off tomorrow."

"Alright, well, you get settled in, and I'll see you in the morning."

He walked to the door. She wanted him to stay but felt uncomfortable with that desire. It had been a long day, sleep would help. With his hand on the doorknob, he turned back. That same look of awe and something else she couldn't place still danced across his features.

"I'll see you tomorrow. Please lock up behind me."

After he left, Julie locked the door.

What a day. Even with the events at the diner, she was feeling grateful, but she was exhausted. She turned off all the lights, except for the bathroom light, which she always left on in a new place, and climbed the stairs to the loft. She crawled into the giant king-size bed. It was soft with warm flannel sheets and a quilt which she snuggled into. Taking a deep breath, Abe's scent was everywhere. Even though he was gone, she could still sense his presence here and that was a comfort to her. She let the day fall away as she drifted off to sleep.

CHAPTER SEVEN

Julie

Julie was up with the sun feeling more refreshed than she had in a long time. That must have been a magical bed. She couldn't recall the last time she slept through the night with no nightmares or uncomfortable springs poking in her back.

She went downstairs and made coffee, then got ready for the day. She found herself at a loss for what to do with her day off. It had been a long time since she hadn't needed to be somewhere or do something for an entire day.

She decided she would repay Abe for his hospitality and the previous evening's dinner with breakfast. She found ingredients for biscuits and gravy and scrambled eggs and set to work. Once the biscuits were out of the oven and the eggs were nearly ready, she walked onto the porch and rang the big triangle.

Within minutes, there was a loud and rapid knock at

the door. It made her jump. She walked over, unlocked the door, and opened it to find a humongous man with panic in his eyes.

"Are you okay?" he asked quickly.

"Yes! I'm fine! I hope I didn't scare you, I just cooked you breakfast since you made me food last night."

"I heard the bell and I got concerned." The panic in his eyes disappeared and a warm smile found his face. He took a big sniff of the air. "It sure does smell good."

"I'm not sure what you like, but I made biscuits and gravy."

"That sounds delicious," he said as he entered. Julie fixed two plates, and they sat down to eat.

"How'd you sleep last night?" he asked.

"Better than I've slept in ages," she replied honestly. They sat together eating and talking. The ease of it all, the food, the conversation, the man beside her, made the short time she'd been here seem far longer.

"I know you don't have to work today, but would you like to go get your car after we finish up here?" Abe asked.

He had no idea how much she wanted that. Her car may be a piece of junk, but it was her piece of junk. There had been many nights where she had nowhere else to go and slept in that car. That car had carried her away from unsafe places. If it hadn't been for Abe and Bridget, her car would have carried her away from Hecate's Hollow two nights ago without looking back. As at home as she felt here in this cabin, she would feel better knowing her car was here and she was free to leave if she needed to.

"Yeah, I'd like that. Thank you," she said with a small smile.

His eyes held her gaze and the look on his face warmed something deep inside of her. For as big and grumpy as he came off, he was a softy inside, she could see that. He was a big part of why she felt safe. That was not a realization she was expecting, but it was there just the same.

After breakfast, they went to the diner to get her car. His blue truck was old, probably from the early '80s, but it seemed to run just fine. It fit his personality. Something about it didn't seem to totally fit into the world around it, but it was big and dependable and made her feel like nothing could harm her.

"Do you mind if we listen to music?" she asked.

They both reached for the dial at the same time. When their hands touched, the same feeling came, but it was stronger, like it had been on the porch that night.

"Do you feel that? What is that?" she asked.

"I do, and I'm not entirely sure."

Whatever it was, it was new and exciting, and a little bit scary. All she knew was she liked being near him. Whatever it was that happened every time they touched was something she hadn't experienced before. It was like this warm tingle that shot through her at the mere touching of their hands, just like it had been last night when their hands had touched in the cabin. And she couldn't even begin to wrap her head around what had happened on the porch between them. Whatever it was she would take it, because being with him like this just felt right.

As they pulled up to the diner, Julie gasped. Her car had been vandalized. The front windshield was broken out and the rest of the car was keyed and spray painted. The sight of her car like that gutted her. It was just a car, it could be fixed, but to Julie it represented so much more than that.

"Wait here," Abe growled. He got out of the truck and stalked over to inspect the car.

Betty came out of the diner and waved to Julie. Julie

gave a small wave; Abe had told her to wait here, and she was going to do just that. He picked up a piece of paper that was under the windshield and went to talk to Betty. After a moment he gave her a few curt nods before making his way back to the truck.

"Betty said it was like this when she opened this morning. Do you want the note?"

She could feel her hands starting to shake. She knew who it was from.

"No. You can read it."

His body tensed as he read.

"He's not fucking getting anywhere near you," he growled.

He slammed his door shut and stalked over to the phone booth.

Julie picked up the note in her trembling hand.

This isn't the end. You owe me and I always get what I'm owed.

Abe got back in the truck. "I have my brother coming to clean up your car right now. He'll move it up to the barn so we can fix it."

"That's not necessary."

"It's done."

And that was all there was to say about that. He wasn't in the mood to talk, which was fine because honestly, neither was she. The ride back to the cabin was a stark comparison to the one to the diner when the little spark glimmered between them. Now everything seemed wrong, except for Abe. Even with seeing her car like that and the fear of what Dale might be capable of, Abe was still gentle and taking care of her. She wasn't used to having someone like him to lean on. It was hard to trust, but it sure did feel good.

When they pulled up to the cabin, they made their way to the porch.

"Do you want to be alone?" he asked.

She didn't. She bit her lip and shook her head.

"Okay, what would you like to do?" he asked with such tenderness it almost broke her.

"Do you want to come inside and watch a movie or something? I just don't want to be alone."

"Of course," said Abe as they walked into the cabin. "Why don't you pick out a movie and I'll make some tea."

Abe had a small shelf of VHS tapes next to the TV which she was surprised by. She picked one out and slid it into the player. It felt good to be back here with Abe, and she didn't really know what to do with those feelings, but they were becoming harder to push away.

He brought her tea and sat at the other end of the couch. She wanted to be there, on his side of the couch and his big safe arms around her. She needed that, but instead, she just took another sip of tea and watched the movie.

About fifteen minutes into the movie, she glanced over again, and once again she caught him looking at her. The pull to be near him was distracting. She took another sip of tea, building up the courage. If she wanted to explore those feelings, it would be up to her. Somehow, she knew he wouldn't push her right now, but the urge she felt to be near him was stronger than almost anything she had ever felt. She just wanted to know what it would feel like.

She shifted her weight to the other end of the couch and snuggled in next to him. "Is this okay?" she asked.

"Yeah," he said with a warm smile. He put his arm around her, and she nestled into him, tucked her feet up underneath her, and rested her head on his shoulder. It felt as good as she'd hoped it would. The feeling that existed between them hummed. After a few minutes, he turned his head to look at her. She looked up into his eyes. Time stopped when she was this close to him. She couldn't help but give a tiny gasp and her lips parted.

He lifted his large hand and delicately tucked a stray bit of hair behind her ear. Their eyes were locked. Her pulse raced and a million butterflies fluttered in her stomach. She wanted to kiss him. She hadn't wanted to kiss anyone in years, but that want was there, and it was bordering on need. Unconsciously, she licked her lips.

His hand that had tucked the hair behind her ear slid so it was cupping her jaw.

"If I'm misreading signals I won't ask again. Can I kiss you?"

She nodded. He bent his head and his lips grazed over hers in the smallest of kisses. The magic that had been humming between them zinged to life and coursed through them. He kissed her again with more intention, and this time she kissed him back. Her hand found his sturdy chest and rested there, and she kissed him again. This time she slightly parted her lips, and he accepted the invitation. His tongue tentatively searched for hers and he kissed slowly. She stilled for a barely perceivable moment waiting for the panic to set it. When it didn't, she deepened the kiss, surprised by the throbbing she felt between her legs.

He stopped kissing her and pulled back to look at her. He was handsome. There was a timeless, ageless quality about him. She was beginning to realize how little she actually knew about this man, but she was dying to know more.

"How long have you lived up here?" she asked.

"My whole life."

"How long is that?"

She could see his mind start to work. She knew he was

older than she was. She was twenty-six so she didn't really care how old he was, but she truly had no idea.

Before he could answer, there was a soft knock at the door. Confusion flooded his face, but he still moved to open it.

CHAPTER EIGHT

Julie

He got up to answer the door and Bridget was standing there with a warm smile.

"Bridget, what are you doing here?" he asked.

"I think we need to talk, Abe," she said with a serious edge to her voice.

He nodded. "Excuse me, Julie," he said to her and moved to step outside.

"No, I think the lass needs to hear this too."

His brow crinkled with concern, but Bridget gently patted his arm. "It'll be alright," she said, giving him a warm smile.

He opened the door, and she came in.

"How about a cuppa tea?" she asked.

"Of course," Abe said as he put the kettle back on and Julie joined them in the kitchen.

"Dear, I heard that terrible man ruined your car," Bridget said with a sympathetic frown.

She nodded. As much as she had been enjoying that moment on the couch with Abe, she was curious why Bridget was here.

Abe finished up the tea and brought it to Bridget. He sat down next to Julie, his big hand finding her thigh, those butterflies began to flutter all over again.

"So, I think the best way to explain this is to come right out and say it --"

"Wait. What are you going to say?" Abe cut her off. He watched her with cautious eyes.

"I'll only reveal my secret," she said. Abe nodded and she continued. "Now, lass, I know the world has been unkind to you, but I've been able to sense great power in you since the moment I first saw you in the diner."

Julie looked at her confused. Power? What on earth was she talking about? Julie had always felt so powerless, so this little Scottish woman telling her she had great power was almost laughable to her.

"I'm sorry. I don't know what you are talking about."

"I know, but I'm going to tell you something, and I'm only letting you in on this little secret because I can see magic in you. I'm a witch, a white witch, a healer is how I started learning about magic. I have since become very powerful, but that's a story for another day."

"I'm sorry, I don't understand," said Julie.

"Aye, I know, dear, but just try and open your mind. I can sense it in you, and Abe can too."

Abe. What did he have to do with this? She looked up at him with a puzzled expression. He looked down at her and nodded.

"That is why I knew I must bring you here and keep you

safe. Dale is no ordinary sleazeball. I imagine you've had your fair share of dealing with men like him, but he's dangerous. I think he can sense your magic too and he won't give up."

Fear began to bubble up inside of her. "What are you talking about?"

"Dale is a warlock. They feed off witch magic. Real witches are not as plentiful as we once were because of all the hunts and conversions. So, when a warlock finds one, especially one with your power, he won't let go easily."

She felt Abe tense next to her. Her eyes danced between Bridget and Abe.

"I think you have something wrong, I'm not magic. There's nothing special about me." She wrung her hands in her lap and looked down. Abe gently put his hand around hers.

"What she says is true, Julie," Abe said. "I can feel it as well. I had some sense of it before Bridget came, I think. But once she came and I started paying attention it became clear. Now I'm not sure how Dale got past me," he said it in almost a growl, eyes on Bridget. Then his gaze softened as he looked back at Julie. "But I do feel magic in you."

"That's not all ya feel, is it, big guy?" Bridget said with a hearty chuckle.

His eyes cut to her with a menacing look.

"I said I wouldn't reveal anything about ye, and I won't. But I'm a matchmaker, let me have my fun," she said. "Lass, can I show ye? I know this is all very new, but if you'll allow me, I can show ye the same way I was shown many years ago."

She turned to Abe. He gave her hand a gentle squeeze and nodded, "It's okay. You can trust Bridget."

"Okay, how are you going to show me?"

"Come outside with me, deary."

They rose from the table and stepped out onto the porch. The rocking chair creaked as she backed into it. Abe steadied her and gave her a warm smile. Looking out, all she saw were the trees whose leaves were starting to turn and the garden patch.

Bridget walked down off the porch and gestured to Julie. "Come here," Bridget said. Julie stepped closer, fear bubbling inside her. Her heart was racing, and her breath was shaky.

"May I take yer hands? Just know, it may change how you see the world around ye, but in the most beautiful way."

Julie reached out her hands and Bridget took them both in her own. It was like the feeling when Abe held her last night, but tenfold. The wind blew around them, but the trees stayed still. She could feel rain on her face, but no rain fell. She could feel the earth move under her feet, but everything remained still. Bridget let go of Julie's hands and stepped back. Julie was left trying to catch her breath.

"What the hell was that?" Julie gasped.

Bridget smiled kindly. "I remember that feeling like it was yesterday, only I was even less prepared for it. That was the magic in you waking up. Look around. Ye may see things a bit differently."

Looking around, she was right, her surroundings looked the same, but different. The plants seemed to be different colors, there were even some plants she had never seen before. She felt like Dorothy when she stepped into munchkin land for the first time; like someone had turned on the colors.

"You're now seeing the magic of the world. We are of

the same magic lineage. You'll be able to use the plants to heal and perform white magic."

"What?" She couldn't stop looking around, everything looked so new and amazing. "I'm a witch?" she pondered out loud.

"Yes, lass, and I'm betting you'll be a powerful one too."

She looked back at Abe and jumped. She saw a large shadow around him. It appeared to be the shadow of a great bear but faded as quickly as it had appeared. Abe was looking at her, his emotion unreadable. She gave a little smile, but he looked away.

"This is what Dale is after, and he won't be easily deterred, but deter him we must. Isn't that right, Abe?" Abe just looked at her with a menacing stare.

"See he agrees, and tell Abe yer not afraid of him, lass."

Abe scowled at her and turned away grumbling.

"What?" Julie asked.

"Just tell him. He could use yer reassurance right now."

"Stop. Bridget," he growled.

"Hey, I've been known to enjoy a good miscommunication trope in my spells, but we don't have time for it right now. We have to catch a warlock." She turned and made her way back to the house.

Did this have to do with the shadow? She reached out and took his hand, "Abe, I'm not afraid of you."

He couldn't meet her eyes.

"Come on you two. We need to devise a trap."

He held the door open, and they entered the kitchen.

"What kind of trap?" Julie asked.

"I imagine if we bring him up here, the mountains themselves may take things from there," Bridget said.

"What do you mean?" asked Julie.

"These mountains are old and there is magic in them

we don't understand. They have a way of dealing with people like him," she said. A gentle breeze blew through the open kitchen window as if on cue.

"How are we going to get him here?" asked Bridget.

"I could deliver him here," Abe grumbled.

"You know you can't do that. That would draw too much attention." Bridget said.

"When I work my shift at the diner, maybe we can lure him then. He might try to follow me here."

"No," Abe growled. "We won't use you as bait."

"Well technically, since she's the one he wants, she *is* bait," Bridget remarked.

"No. I won't put her in any more danger."

While she did like the feeling of being protected for once, she'd taken care of herself for nearly ten years.

"I can do it," Julie said. "I'll just go back to working at the diner. I'll let you know if he is there."

"No." He said it as if it were the end of the idea.

"No?" she balked.

"No," he said plainly.

"I've been taking care of myself for a long time now. While I appreciate your concern, I can do this."

He glowered at her, but she wouldn't back down.

"Now, I'm rarely one to interject in a lover's quarrel, but Julie will draw Dale here, regardless. We can, however, choose the time and manner of his approach and how prepared we are."

Abe took a deep, rumbly breath but didn't protest any further.

"I'm supposed to work the lunch shift Thursday, but then on Friday I am closing, maybe we can try then."

"I think that works. The moon is full on Saturday, so he'll be wanting to get you then, when your powers will be ripe for the taking. Not to mention it's a blue moon on the eve of Samhain."

Abe nodded but was still clearly not fully on board. "We'll have eyes on her the whole time."

"Not the whole time," she protested.

"The whole time." His eyes bore into her.

"If he sees you there, he'll know something's up," Julie protested.

"She does have a point, Abe," said Bridget. Abe puffed his chest ready to protest, but Bridget put her hand on his shoulder. "But I agree with Abe. We'll have eyes on you the whole time. They may just be harder to see. The diner butts up against the forest. I believe we know some people who can stay hidden in the forest with sharp senses."

Abe nodded through a glower, but Bridget continued nonplussed. "So, you take care of that how you will. I'll work some magic to help the mountain along."

Bridget stood. "Right then, I'm off. I'll see you tomorrow. I'm sure Abe will make sure the diner is safe, and we'll proceed with the plan. Now, this isn't how I normally work, but I'm going to need you two to figure some stuff out quickly. You two are clearly a soul match. I know it. Abe knows it. And I'm sure you have some sense of it, Julie. Normally I like to plant the seed, watch it unfold, and throw in some chaos for my own amusement, but there simply is no time. If we are going to trap a desperate warlock, we need all of our collective heads in the game. So, figure it out."

"Goodbye Bridget," Abe said, walking her to the door.

That last part had pulled Julie up short. What did she mean by soul match? That sounded an awful lot like not having a choice. That is precisely what she had been running from all these years. Men holding claim over her.

She belonged to her father until the day she would be given to her husband. Then he would possess her to do with as he pleased. She would never go back to that. She would live her own life and make her own choices. And if the way he had just behaved was any indication, Abe may have some control issues, and she was not going to live under the control of another man. Ever.

Her pulse quickened until it pounded in her head. Her breathing became quick and short. She couldn't shake the sensation of the walls closing in. She knew this feeling; she was having a panic attack.

Abe shut the door behind Bridget and turned to face her.

"Julie, are you okay?"

She should answer him, but the tightness in her chest and the pounding in her head stopped any words from coming. She closed her eyes and tried to focus on her breathing.

"Julie..." he sat next to her and looked at her. "How can I help you?"

But at that moment she was gone. She was deep in her trauma. The feeling of helplessness and hopelessness gripped her. She had lived her life at the whim of men. They always had the ultimate control.

She was vaguely aware of Abe's big hand taking hers.

"Julie, I think you're having a panic attack. I'm here with you."

She sat there trembling, eyes closed tight and lost in fear.

"I'm here," he said between slow deliberate breaths. "You are safe."

Julie found herself reflexively matching his breathing. Her pulse fell and the panic subsided. She eventually managed to open her eyes. He was there. His eyes were full of kindness and patience. He continued his deep breathing with her clammy, trembling hands in his. She gave him a weak smile.

"Thank you."

He nodded and gave her hand a little squeeze.

For a moment she just sat there. That was a lot to take in: Witch? Fine. Warlock after her? Fine. Soul-bound to another human? Panic. That was not a normal reaction.

"Abe, what did she mean by soul match?"

Abe looked down at his hands. He took a deep breath.

"Bridget's favorite magic is matchmaking. She's probably the most powerful magical creature I've ever encountered in my existence, but she uses it only to bring together people who she can see as soulmates. But that's all it is, matchmaking."

She could see the uncertainty in his eyes. She was used to seeing him strong and steady, but he looked vulnerable and afraid. On instinct, Julie laced her fingers in his. A small smile found his face.

"This whole day is a lot to take in. Learning I'm a witch and that there is a warlock after me is a lot. I don't think it's really sunk in yet. But I do feel what she was talking about between us, and I'm being honest with you, that scares me more than the warlock."

He was silent for a moment. "Can I ask why?"

This wasn't something she normally talked about. In fact, it was something she never talked about, but it was now or never.

"Yeah...but you're going to have to bear with me. I've never really talked to anyone about this."

He brought his other hand up. Both of his hands were holding hers and he patiently waited for her to continue.

"I was raised in a conservative home with an abusive father. We were just supposed to take it and not ask any questions. He spoke to God and beat us whenever we got out of line." She could feel him stiffen next to her, but he didn't interrupt. "When I was seventeen, I got pregnant. I didn't even know what sex was. My boyfriend told me what we were doing was fine. Since I had always been raised to listen to men, I didn't speak up for myself, even though I knew in my gut something wasn't right. Anyway, the day my father found out I was pregnant was the last day I spoke to him. He kicked me out of the house with nothing. My boyfriend was going to go with me, and we were going to live together, but then the church 'brought him back into the fold.' I was blamed for it entirely. He was too scared to go against them, so he gave me enough money to get an abortion and a place to stay for a month. But after that, I was on my own."

Finally, she looked over at him. She had been staring down at the table while recounting her past. There was so much shame for her.

"I'm sorry those things happened to you." He was calm and accepting, and she didn't know why that brought back some of the panic.

"I don't regret my choices. Any of them. I couldn't have cared for a baby with the life I live. It's been hard. There have been times I've been homeless. I've been hungry. I've been attacked. But I've survived. Because of that past, it's very hard for me to trust people, especially men."

He nodded and continued listening.

"While I do feel drawn to you and so incredibly safe with you, I'm nervous about being bound to a man. Does that make sense?"

"Yes. It makes sense. I feel drawn to you too. I trust

Bridget and her magic. But I need you to know, even if we are soulmates, you are free. You're not bound to me. I'd never hurt you or control you. I'd gladly lay the heart of the warlock at your feet, but only if you wish. I promise, you're safe here. And while I may over-step when it comes to your safety, I'll never take away your choice over anything pertaining to your body, your space, or your freedom."

Looking into his eyes calmed her a bit. There was so much sincerity behind them. She knew in her core that she could trust him. She was safe with him. Those were new feelings her mind was still trying to reject, even though her heart knew them to be true.

"I believe you, but please be patient with me."

"Endlessly."

"I told you about my past. Will you show me the same honesty?" She asked.

"Yes. I ask you to have an open mind and know this doesn't change anything about me."

She nodded.

"I could tell when Bridget awakened your sight that you saw something around me. While I'm not sure what you saw, I have a guess. I just don't want you to be afraid of me. My family and I have lived in these mountains for a long time. We are the magic keepers. Most of the women in my family are witches, but it works a little differently for men."

She gave him a small smile and waited for him to continue.

"Part of being a protector is being given an animal form. I believe you saw part of my animal form on the porch...Did you see something?"

She nodded.

"What did you see?"

"I saw the shadow of a bear around you."

"Yes, so you know my animal form."

"So, you change into a bear? When you are a bear do you have any control over things? Like how you change and all of that?" she asked.

"I have complete control over those things. Always."

"So, you aren't dangerous?"

"I'm no danger to you." He reached out and tentatively took her hand. She was relieved that the magic that danced between them was still there and not overpowered by the panic she had felt moments ago. She held onto it tightly. "I may be dangerous to that warlock, but never to you."

Contentment settled inside of her. Knowing she had someone like Abe on her side felt good. Not only did she not have to face these new challenges on her own, but she had someone who she could count on and who would protect her. She had protected herself as best she could for years, and she knew she could do so, but being able to relax for once felt nice. And while it might not quite be time to relax fully, she knew the time was coming if she and Abe were truly meant to be together.

CHAPTER NINE

Abe

"Julie are you okay?" he asked with kindness filling his voice.

"Yeah, I think it's all just catching up with me. The attack at the diner and my car, those things all suck, but nothing I haven't dealt with before. But all this stuff today with the magic and everything else, and the panic attack. I think I just need a minute."

"Of course, it is a lot to take in. I'll let you have some time." Abe stood to leave, but Julie reached out and grabbed his hand. Once again, he could feel their magic dancing. His magic seemed to yearn for her just as much as he did.

"Don't go," she protested, her voice barely above a whisper.

"If you do not wish me to leave, I won't." His thumb lightly rubbed the hand he was still holding.

"Can we just watch the movie? I just want to pretend

like I don't know any of that stuff until I figure out how to deal with it."

"We can do that," he said as he helped her to stand.

They made their way back over to the couch. This time Julie made no pretense to even trying to sit on the other side. He sat down and she snuggled right into him and started the movie up. He pulled the Afghan from the back of the couch to cover her. She gave a contented sigh and snuggled in. Abe loved every minute of it.

He had never felt the pull to anyone like he had felt to her. If he had given it thought, he would have realized who she was a long time ago, but what would he have done with that information? He was a loner. He had his brother, but that was it. Asher would go into town, he had friends there and participated in town events, but Abe chose to be by himself. Live his life in his cabin like the creature of comfort he was. But now, he had her to worry about, and worried he was.

He had been drawn to Julie the few interactions he'd had at the diner, but when Bridget arrived, it changed. When he was more connected to his magic, he could clearly see her magic before Bridget even brought her up on his mountain. Maybe it was the disconnect from his magic that made him overlook Julie and Dale. He was still trying to figure out how there had been a warlock in their midst and neither him nor Asher had been aware. Either of them should have been able to detect him from miles away. But that was a problem for another day, right now he was more than happy to focus on the girl snuggling into him on the couch.

Her hand rested on his thigh and her head was on his chest. His arm wrapped around her and was lightly drawing circles on her arm. A small sigh escaped her mouth, and he gave her a little squeeze. She looked up at him and smiled with those big green eyes, and he knew he would do anything for her. He wanted her by his side, and he hadn't felt that way until now.

She reached up and kissed him. It was a chaste kiss, but there was so much tenderness behind it.

"Thank you, Abe," she said so softly he barely heard her over the movie.

"Whatever for?"

"For giving me a place to stay. For being so understanding. You're the first man I've ever felt safe around. I don't think I realized how much I needed that."

"I want you to feel safe. This is your home for as long as you need it. You're safe here. The woods are protected. No one can find us on this mountain unless they're shown the way. It is part of the magic that protects us. And I'll make sure you're safe at the diner until this whole warlock business is behind us," he said as he brushed a lock of hair behind her ear.

She reached her face up to his and gave him another quick kiss before settling her head back down on his chest to watch the movie. He inhaled a deep breath, taking in her scent. Her shampoo smelled of almonds and honey. Amusement danced across his face. She really was his perfect match, smelling of honey and all.

His mind wandered to where else she might smell like honey, but that was not a thought for this moment. He was incredibly attracted to her, but he wouldn't rush this. He could tell she was someone who needed time, someone who didn't trust easily. He would gladly spend the time earning that trust. If he had his way, he would spend his whole life earning and keeping her trust. It felt a little too early to be planning what a life on this mountain would look like with her, but he couldn't stop himself. She was it for him, and if he hadn't been avoiding it, he would have known well before now.

Before long he noticed her breathing had become slow and rhythmic and that she was laying very still. Glancing down he found her eyes were closed, and she looked peaceful. He was glad she was sleeping; it had been a very eventful day for her. And really, she had taken all the new information like a champ.

There was a soft knock at the door. He quickly tried to stealthily get out from underneath her. He propped her head up on a pillow. The door opened with a creak as he was getting out from under Julie. Asher was standing in the door frame with a smile stretched across his face.

"Hey, I just wanted to check--"

"Shh," Abe said and pointed to the porch.

The two men stepped outside, and Abe shut the door behind him, careful not to make a sound. Asher had wagged his eyebrows at Abe.

"Looks like someone is going to wifey up," he said, trying to get a rise out of Abe.

"Shut the fuck up. We have a bigger problem than you being a dumb ass," Abe said with a frown.

"Oh yeah?"

"Bridget left not too long ago. Do you know that guy Dale from the motel?"

"Yeah, he's the scum of the earth, man," Asher said.

"You can say that again. He's the one who attacked her last night and the one who did that to her car."

"I'm not surprised. Are we kicking his ass?"

"We might be doing more than that. I found out why Bridget is staying at the motel."

Asher cocked his eyebrow waiting for Abe's to continue.

"He's a fucking warlock," Abe growled out.

"Are you serious? There hasn't been a warlock here in Hecate's Hollow since mama and dad were still in charge. How did he go unnoticed this long?"

"I don't know, and there's one more thing..."

Asher gestured for Abe to continue.

"Julie's a witch. That's why Dale is after her."

Asher's eyes turned menacing, and a growl rumbled his chest.

"My sentiments exactly, brother. There is a plan to lure him here and let the woods have him, but we're going to need your help."

"If it involves ripping a warlock to shreds, I'm in."

"That's the end goal, but I need eyes and ears on Julie while she's at the diner. Bridget seems to think he'll follow her home Friday night on the blue moon. So, that night I'll be outside the diner, and I thought you could run a perimeter and make sure he doesn't get on the mountain. And the day before that maybe you eat at the diner and shift and hang out in the woods behind it. I'll be there."

"You got it. I can't believe we didn't know he was a warlock," Asher said, shaking his head.

"Well after Esther left, then Sunny, there were no witches in Hecate's Hollow. He didn't show himself, but when Julie showed up right on his doorstep. I'm just glad he was waiting until the blue moon to try and get as much power as he can."

"I'm glad Bridget showed up. So, is Julie your mate?"

"You read too many romance novels; you know she's not my mate."

"Okay, but you know what I mean. What did Bridget have to say about it?"

Abe took a deep breath. He did not want to talk about this with his brother.

"I thought so," Asher said with a face full of gloat.

"Abe," Julie's sleepy voice called from inside.

"Wait here," Abe said. But Asher wasn't having that. He followed Abe right into his cabin.

"Hey Julie, it's ok. I was just outside talking to my brother," he said with a small smile. "Who I told to stay outside," he whispered harshly back to his brother.

"Asher. I didn't realize you were Abe's brother. Are you a bear too?"

"Nope, Abe's the only bear in these parts." Julie gave him a small nod. "I'm a wolf, which makes me at least ten times cooler."

"You're an idiot," Abe said flatly behind his brother.

"Abe was catching me up on all the warlock plans. Don't worry Julie, we got you."

"Thanks. Would you guys like some dinner? I can see what there is to cook if you're hungry."

"That's not necessary," said Abe. While Asher said, "Fantastic."

Julie looked between the two brothers and laughed. "I'll make dinner. It's the least I can do for the trouble I have brought to you."

"No trouble, Julie. I'm ready for a good warlock hunt," grinned Asher.

After dinner, Asher and Abe took off to the other cabin. Part of Abe wanted Julie to ask him to stay. She might have asked him if Asher hadn't been there, but it worked out better this way. She could use a little time to digest all the information she had been given today. Still, he found himself missing her.

CHAPTER TEN

Julie

Julie woke up the next morning after yet another restful sleep inside the cozy little cabin. That kind of surprised her after the events of the past couple days. From the incident in the diner, to her car, and then of course, there was the fact that she was a witch and there was a warlock after her. Those things all seem completely unreal, but oddly she had no trouble believing them. The one that was throwing her the most was that she shared a soul connection with a bear shifter, and it wasn't even the fact that he was a bear shifter that was throwing her.

She buried her face in a pillow and groaned. What was wrong with her? Why was she so scared of having a connection like that with Abe? She did feel that connection to him, she felt very drawn to him and safe with him. She also was attracted to him in a way she had never been attracted to anyone before. The way she felt when she touched him was nothing she had ever experienced, yet the idea that she shared that type of bond with a man scared her.

She knew part of it was because of her past. Living her life under the control of men for so long had been hard. To her family, she was a daughter who was there to do the will of her father until it would be time for her to be married, then she would be there to be at the will of her husband, and that scared her even more.

Life had been hard when she was kicked out of that community, the struggle was real, and it was heavy. But she was free, well as free as you can be in a harsh world. The idea of depending on someone else scared her.

Once she was out on her own so much of the world opened to her. In her parents' home there was no TV, no friends outside of their faith, no outside 'corrupting' influence of any kind. She had known nothing about the world around her. She knew nothing about sex, which is how she wound up pregnant in the first place. She knew nothing about pop culture. She knew nothing about actual science, even actual history. Her entire life had been distorted through the lens of fundamentalism.

After ten years on her own, she was starting to figure stuff out. When she had first left, she just holed herself up in the hotel room her boyfriend had paid for she watched tv for the first time. There was a marathon of the Designing Women on, and she just laid in bed watching it. These women were all so strong and independent. She never knew life could be like that. It gave her hope that she would be able to be like them. She wanted to be Julia Sugarbaker. She wanted to help people and give them a voice and be fierce, but she had no idea how to do any of those things.

And then as life went on, she gave up on those dreams and realized she would be lucky just to survive. She found she was a pretty good waitress. It seems fitting because serving people was all she had ever been trained to do anyway, so it came easy to her.

Her first job was waiting tables at the twenty-four-hour diner next to the first motel she stayed in. She was there for a while, and even saved up enough to buy a car. Things were falling into place, that was until the owner of the diner retired and left the business to his son.

She had always steered clear of him because he gave her creepy vibes. One night when it was just the two of them in the diner, he had tried to force himself on her. When she fought back, he fired her. After that she could no longer pay for the motel room, so she stayed in her car. She moved on to the next small town and got a job at a diner there.

That was how it had been ever since. Staying at a place until it had proven to be unsafe, scraping and saving to barely squeak by. Her car had been the only real thing she had ever bought. While it was an old piece of junk to some people, to her it had been her saving grace more than once. It had been a place to weather the storm when she had nowhere else to go. It had been her getaway car when she needed to escape another dangerous situation. It had been everything. When she saw it yesterday morning all spray painted and keyed and the windows broken out, it felt like even more of a violation.

Being violated in one way or another had been happening to her for her entire life. She never had her own agency. That was why the idea of being soul bound to another person was so terrifying. She needed to be able to get away if the time came, and being bound to another person made that escape more complicated.

But as she looked around this room, she could almost feel Abe here with her. She wanted Abe here with her. She wanted his quiet and calming presence. She wanted to be wrapped up in his big strong arms. But there was a part of her that pumped those brakes because that was so much power to give over to another person.

Still, she made her way downstairs and started getting breakfast. She had one more day off before she would work the lunch shift at the diner. As she got the coffee maker going, she took a moment to look around the cabin. Yesterday she had thought all the bear carvings and the painting were just basic rustic cabin decoration, but now they made her smile.

She did have a lot of questions now that everything had begun to sink in. Like, did he have control over when he shifted? Could he only shift at certain times? What kind of bear was he? The idea of cuddling with an actual bear made her smile. Never in a million years would she have thought anything like this was possible.

Then there was the fact that she was magic. It did explain a lot though when she thought about it. This one had a lot of weird fundamentalist shame with it. Being a witch would have been seen as being a part of the devil himself. She had unpacked enough of her religious trauma to know she didn't believe in all that stuff. She didn't believe in heaven and hell. She wasn't even sure how she felt about God. She knew she believed in something, but she didn't know what to call it. Magic was as good an explanation as any she guessed.

Bridget had said she would stop by today and answer some questions and teach her about magic. She was looking forward to that. Bridget had shown her the world in this new way, awoken her magic, as she had put it. Learning more about it was something she was looking forward to.

She poured herself a cup of coffee and got to work making breakfast. After a while there was a soft knock at the door. Her heart leapt, but in a nice fluttery way, not in the anxiety filled way of before. She knew who was on the other side of that door and she was excited to see him.

As she opened the door, she saw Abe there on the other side.

"This is your house. You don't have to knock," she said. The bashful feeling she felt surprised her, but she did feel kind of bumbling at the moment.

He smiled at her and ran his hand through his hair, he seemed to be feeling as bashful as she was. They were quite a pair, a witch and a bear with poor social skills fighting feelings for each other. Part of her just wanted to give up the fight and fall into his arms. The kiss they had shared yesterday before this all got even more complicated had been nice. It had been very nice. It had been one of the nicest things in her life, and she was looking forward to kissing him again.

"I told you, this is your house while you're here." Their eyes connected as he stood there in the doorway, the connection they both felt was heavy in the air. "Can I come in?"

"Oh! Of course! Sorry, yes, come in. I just finished up breakfast if you're hungry," she said as she made her way over to the little kitchen to fix him a plate.

"How did you sleep?" he asked as he sat down at the table.

"Good, surprisingly good."

The warm smile he gave her lit a small glow inside of her. She sighed and smiled at him.

"Your car should be all set for tomorrow. Asher and I got it all sanded last night and replaced the window that was broken. What color do you want it? We can match the old green if you want it the same, but it's up to you," he said as he ate a forkful of scrambled eggs.

"Really? I can pick any color?" she said excitedly.

"Any color the auto store has," he said.

"Can it be red?"

"You got it."

"I've always wanted a red car," she said with a grin on her face.

"Then red you shall have," he said with a head nod. "I was wondering if you would be interested in a walk through the woods. If you're not interested, that's fine. Or if you have business in town, I can run you in. It's up to you."

"I would love to take a walk in the woods with you, Abe."

"Well, let me help you clean up breakfast and we'll head out."

After the dishes were done and Julie had changed into her most appropriate hiking clothes, they set out for a walk in the woods. The moment they opened the door, Julie was once again shocked at the way everything had changed for her since Bridget had awakened her magic.

The colors were more vibrant. Everything was just turned up and she was excited to know what all of it meant.

"Does everything look colorful to you?" she asked him.

"What do you mean?"

"I don't know how to explain it, but after whatever Bridget did yesterday, things look different. The plants are more colorful, some of them different colors, some of them glow," she said as she looked around.

"Nothing glows. I can't really say much about the colors because everything is the way it always has been for me. I became a shifter when I was a teenager, and nothing changed then. But I would imagine since you are a white witch, certain plants show up differently because of their healing properties. My mom was a white witch before she died."

They walked in silence down a path. Julie wanted to ask about his parents. She wanted to ask about him and his brother and if they had any more relatives and if they did, were they magic too? But she didn't want to pry, so they just walked in silence until they came to a little stream. The plants here were like nothing Julie had ever seen before. It was beautiful. There was even a swing on one of the branches of a tree near the stream.

"This place is amazing," she said with wide eyes.

Abe took a deep breath and looked around. "Yeah, this is one of my favorite places. My mom used to come here all the time to collect herbs and my brother and sister and I would take turns on the swing or splashing in the stream."

"You have a sister?"

"A twin sister," he said with a nod.

"Really? Does she live around here too?"

"No, she lives in Tennessee. She got married and left. She didn't really like living in Hecate's Hollow. I haven't seen her in a long time."

Julie couldn't imagine wanting to leave here. She had only stayed here for two nights, but already this place felt more like a home than any place she had ever been. This idyllic little spot next to a stream was right out of a postcard, but now that she was seeing things differently it was more beautiful than anything she had seen before.

"I wonder what these plants do?" she asked as she ran her hands over some green leaves with blue flowers, as she did all this little golden fleck started to fly around the plants before landing back on the leaves.

"I'm not sure. Bridget will be able to answer some of those questions for you later today."

The swing looked so inviting. She couldn’t remember the last time she had been on a swing. She pulled on it slightly to test its strength.

"Get on," Abe said as he steadied the ropes.

"No, it won't hold me," she said. Abe just looked at her with a raised eyebrow before moving in front of the swing and sitting on it. The branch only moved slightly under his weight, and he was much bigger than she was. He stood and moved behind it, holding it steady for Julie to get on.

Julie settled on the swing and was surprised by the sturdiness. Then Abe's hands gave her a gentle push. Even at that small contact she felt the spark dance between them. No one had pushed her on a swing in years, decades even. The wind blew through her hair, and she couldn't remember feeling this free and this safe ever in her life. Maybe being soul bound to this incredible man wouldn't be too bad. She couldn't help but laugh as she was pushed higher and out over the water a little bit.

"You have an amazing laugh," Abe said as he pushed.

This moment was perfect. Here she was with her world turned upside down and a warlock after her. But this man, who had shown her such kindness, was pushing her on a swing, and it felt amazing. With each push, all the doubts she felt earlier fell away. This free feeling taking hold of her was what she had been hoping for her whole life, and here it was. The emotions she was being swept away in took her by surprise. She quickly wiped a tear away.

Abe's pushes slowed, he seemed to be able to sense the emotions she was being swept away in. "Julie, are you okay?"

He stopped the swing and came around standing in

front of her and wiped away the tear that had found its way down her cheek and she smiled up at him.

"What's wrong?" he asked with such tenderness.

"Nothing." He gave her a look telling her he wasn't buying it. "No, really. I feel good. I feel safe and free, things I haven't felt for a long time."

The hand that had wiped away the tear was still cupping her jaw. His thumb gently rubbed her cheek, and it lit a fire deep inside of her. She turned her face and kissed his hand. She wasn't sure why she had done it and it surprised her, but it felt right. This felt right being here with him, more right than anything had felt in her entire life.

She looked up at his face and suddenly she found it hard to breathe. Her heart was pounding and there was an unfamiliar throbbing between her legs. The energy flowing between them was palpable. A strong gust came through the woods, and it seemed to lift her off the swing and right into Abe's arms.

She reached up on her tiptoes and threw her arms around his neck and kissed him. This kiss was different from the one they had shared yesterday. That kiss had been soft and exploratory, this kiss was filled with more heat. It stirred up a desire in her she didn't know she had.

Abe stopped and pulled away and Julie almost whined with need. These were big new feelings, and she wasn't quite sure what to do with them. "Julie, is this what you want?" he asked. His hands found her waist and Julie wasn't sure of much, but she was sure she wanted this man.

She nodded and reached back to kiss him.

"Julie, you have to tell me. I know you've had a rough past and I don't want you to feel pressured by what you learned yesterday." He held her gaze with an intensity that almost took her breath away.

"I'm not sure of much, Abe, but I am sure that I want to kiss you right now. Please kiss me."

And then his arms slid around her waist and his lips found hers and she was on fire. His lips pressed firmly against hers and his arms held her close to his big body. Her hands trailed up his big arms and the muscles there made her stomach tighten a bit. Even when she had kissed other men in the past, she had never been filled with this much desire.

A small moan escaped her mouth as she wrapped her arms around his neck and pressed herself against him. His mouth parted and she opened to him. His tongue slowly began to explore her mouth.

She broke the kiss but stayed pressed against him. Her head found its place on his big chest. She took a deep breath as she melted into him, the softness of his worn flannel shirt against her face. His big hands rubbed her back. He smelled like the woods, fresh and green and earthy. She just wanted to bury her face in his chest and never leave. As he held her and the rest of the world seemed to fall away, she became very aware of his heartbeat, matching hers perfectly.

She still wasn't quite sure what she wanted or how to feel about everything she had found out yesterday, but here in this moment it all fell away, and it was just her and Abe. It was just her and this kind man who had saved her in more than one way, and she wanted it to last forever. Forget all the complications of the world around them, and just live here in the forest.

CHAPTER
ELEVEN

Julie

The perfect moment between Abe was interrupted by an unexpected laugh. Julie jumped in his arms and turned to see Bridget leaning up against a tree smiling at them.

"I see you are taking me up on my advice to get a jump on the soul match," Bridget said to them with a Cheshire Cat grin.

"That's enough, Bridget. Please don't make Julie feel awkward about this. It's counterproductive to your plan," he said dryly.

"Alright, alright! How are ye feeling this morning, Julie? Ye had quite a lot to think about last night."

Turning to face Bridget, Abe's hand found its spot on the small of her back and rubbed a small circle.

"I mean... good, I guess. I still don't know if it's all sunk in yet."

"I can imagine the shock. I remember it like it was yesterday when I found out about magic in the forest with my darling Fergus. I'm here to answer any questions you may have. And it's good that I found you two here. This was one of the places I was going to take you today. Ruth planted lots of medicinal herbs in this part of the stream."

"I would love to know what some of these are. I don't think I've ever seen some of these before."

"Yes, lass. I'll tell you what I can. Abe, Asher was looking for you. He said he's ready to paint the car, but he didn't know what color."

"Did you still want red?" he asked.

"Yeah, I'd like that," she said softly, biting back a grin. Something about looking into his eyes felt different now and it made her melt into him, but they weren't alone, so she pushed that away for now.

"Okay, I'll let him know. Bridget, I trust you can show her back to the cabin?"

"Abe, of course! I know my way around these woods. I walked them often enough with your mother."

"Are you good if I take off? I want to help Asher get your car done so you have it for tomorrow."

Julie couldn't help but smile at the warm look in his eyes. The thought that if she said, 'I'd rather you stay with me' and she knew without a doubt he would, settled her. He would send Bridget to tell Asher what color to paint the car and they could go right back to the wonderful moment they were having before Bridget came. As good as that sounded, she did have as many questions for Bridget as she did for Abe.

"Go ahead, I think Bridget and I have some things to talk about."

"Okay, I'll meet you up at the cabin later," he said before

he bent to kiss her head. The simpleness of that gesture made her smile. Many things felt out of control and new right now, but whatever it was between Abe and Julie felt simple and true. She just wanted to be near him.

He walked away and Julie couldn't help but smile as he seemed to lumber through the forest. He was at home here and she found herself wanting to be at home with him here too.

"I see you and Abe are getting on with things," Bridget said with a warm smile.

Julie bit her lip, holding in a smile, and nodded her head. "I've never met anyone like him before."

"Aye, he's one of a kind. That's for sure."

"How long have you known him?"

"I've known Abe his entire life. I was a friend of his mother's. She was a powerful witch. I wish she was here. I know she could teach you some things even I can't teach you."

"I'm excited to learn anything you can teach me. I still can't believe I'm a witch."

"It is hard to believe at first, but I can help you where I can. This is the place where Ruth planted a lot of herbs. She told me she planted them here because plants that grow near water had stronger magic. This one here is mugwort, it can be used for digestive issues, but it can also help women trying to conceive to have regular cycles."

Bridget showed her a couple other plants and told her their uses. Julie nodded, trying to tuck away that knowledge, though she didn't know how she was going to remember all of this.

"Why don't we head back to the cabin. There are many other wonderful little magic plants there and along the way. I also have a little something to give you."

They made their way back to the cabin and Bridget continued pointing out magic herbs and their remedies. There was no way she would be able to remember all of this, but it was interesting, nonetheless. She was excited to learn more and see what she could do.

"I'm really enjoying my time with ye today, Julie," Bridget said as the cabin was coming into view. "It reminds me of Scotland. I spent many happy years there in my own little cabin in the woods with my Fergus. I helped many people with all sorts of ailments. You'll find most people come to you for matters of the heart and for help to conceive bairns or help with bairns they aren't yet ready for."

"I think I'd like to help people with all of those things," Julie said. Part of the reason she found herself without a home was because of an unwanted pregnancy. She never felt bad about her choice, and the idea that she could support women in that choice did make her feel better.

Bridget showed her a couple more plants that were around the cabin.

"Do these plants grow everywhere?"

"I think you could find them in most places, but this mountain is special. The plants here are more powerful than anywhere else. In fact, I need to talk to Abe about collecting and drying some to refill my personal stash."

There was a gentle breeze through the trees that seemed to caress Julie, almost welcoming her home.

"What do you mean this is a magical place? I can feel it, but why is there more magic than anywhere else?"

"There are spots where the magic is more powerful all over. I grew up near a similar place in Scotland. There are many of them and each is a little different from the next.

This is a place for earth magic and there is also a fair amount of dark magic here."

"Dark magic? Is that something to be worried about?"

"No, my dear. That's not how magic works. Magic is not solely good or evil, it all depends on who wields it. Has Abe told you about his sister?"

"Just that he had a twin sister, but she left when she got married."

"She'll be back. But anyway, she is a powerful dark witch, but she would never harm anyone. It is all about balance. We need the light to balance the dark, life to balance death, both are sides of the same coin. There is a time for all magic."

"How do you know so much about Appalachian Magic if you are from Scotland?"

"Well, Ruth taught me quite a bit, but Scottish and Appalachian white magic are very similar. A long time ago many, Scots settled in these mountains after being kicked out of their ancestral land. The magic they brought with them married with the magic traditions that were already here making it a style of magic all its own, but one whose roots feel very familiar to me."

"That's really interesting."

Bridget climbed the stairs as Julie was still taking everything in. "Come inside with me, lass. I have something for you."

"You didn't have to do that," Julie replied quickly.

"Nonsense, come inside."

Julie followed Bridget in the cabin and there on the table was a big leather-bound book.

"What's that?"

"That, lass, is a grimoire."

"And what is a grimoire?"

Bridget picked up the book and handed it to her. "Take a look. A grimoire is a place for a witch to keep all of her spells and incantations."

Julie took the book from her and could feel the weight of it in her hand. This wasn't a flimsy notebook, but a big well-made journal. She untied the strips of leather that were holding it closed. Setting it down on the table she opened the pages.

"I went ahead and put in the plants we talk about today and the uses they have. But from this point on, this book is only for you."

"This is incredible. I'm not even sure what to do with this. How will I learn things?"

"Well, I'll be around for a couple weeks, and I can help ye, but now that yer on this path, that book will fill itself as ye go about things."

"Like really fill itself?"

Bridget chuckled. "No, my dear, ye will fill it out. I just mean you'll meet people who'll share little bits of magic with you. You'll learn more with the herbs and how your magic works with them. You'll perfect recipes and grow your craft. All of that you'll put in here."

"Thank you so much, Bridget. This is amazing."

"Why don't I put the kettle on and make us a nice cuppa tea? Then ye can ask me any other questions ye have."

And she did, and they spent the next couple hours talking about magic and herbs and their past.

Julie leafed through the book while Bridget got some tea on. It was fascinating. There was so much to learn. Bridget had drawn each plant, common uses, and ways to use them for each of the different herbs. There was also a small section on local folklore. She was looking forward to reading this in full. There was so much to learn, and she found herself wanting to use it all.

Bridget came and set another cup of tea beside her, and she kept reading. As scary as some of the things that she had learned in the last twenty-four hours had been, this was something that felt right. And she couldn't help but smile to herself when she thought about Abe. He felt pretty right too. This whole life that was being offered to her felt too good to be true. She wasn't quite sure if she could trust it yet, but she wanted to.

She was pulled out of her book when the door opened. Abe and Asher walked in talking. Asher carried a Tupperware container that looked like it was full of some marinating meat.

"I got some venison steaks to toss on the grill. Sound good?" Asher announced to the room.

"Sounds good to me," Julie said looking up, her eyes connected with Abe's, and he gave her a small smile.

"Sounds good to me too," said Bridget. "I'll go outside with you and get the grill going." She hooked her arm through Asher's and winked at Abe on her way out.

"Subtlety had never been one of Bridget's strengths," Abe said, walking over to the table where Julie was still pouring over her grimoire.

"I can see that about her."

Abe pulled out a chair next to her and sat down. "What's that?"

"Bridget gave it to me. She wrote all the plants she showed me today and what they do, the rest is for me to fill out. It's all starting to feel more real."

"How are you feeling about that?"

Her bottom lip caught between her teeth as she looked up at Abe. She was almost afraid talking about it out loud would jinx it. The look in his eyes did make her feel safe, and this place did feel like home, and these people were starting to feel like family.

"Surprisingly enough, I feel pretty good about it, warlock aside."

"You don't need to worry about him. We have him handled...or at least we will." He tucked a strand of hair behind her ear and the glow inside she felt whenever he was near was warming her from the inside out.

The door opened. "We got your car all painted, Julie," Asher said. "It should be good as new after it dries. I can bring it down here tomorrow morning if that works." He joined them at the table, unaware of the moment he had just interrupted. That was until he noticed Abe's displeased grimace.

"Thank you so much," Julie said, before Abe could say anything to his brother. "It really means a lot to me. Me and that car have a long history."

Bridget came over to join them.

For the rest of the night, the four of them shared a meal and stories. Asher and Bridget were good story tellers, and it was easy. Julie had never felt this comfortable around people before. Growing up there was a constant fear of messing up, here she just felt accepted. And the fact that Abe's hand was resting on her knee under the table rubbing a small circle with her thumb made her feel like she was glowing from the inside out.

"Alright Asher, why don't we get out of here?" Bridget asked. "You can walk me back to my car so I can get back to the disgusting motel to keep an eye on our warlock."

"Yep, let's do it. See you tomorrow, Julie," he said, giving her an easy smile.

"See ya later."

Bridget and Asher walked out together, leaving Abe and Julie alone. "I was wondering if you wanted to take a walk with me," she said with a hint of shyness in her voice.

"I would love to." He smiled at her and grabbed her lightweight sweatshirt off the rack by the door and held it out for her. She slipped it on as Abe opened the door.

They set off walking down a path she hadn't been down yet.

"There's a nice view this way," he said, offering his hand.

She reached out and his big hand wrapped around hers. His hand was giant compared to hers, yet another thing about this man that made her feel safe. The callouses, the size, the neat clean trimmed nails, all of it made her feel safe.

The sun was low in the sky and with the colored leaves just starting to fall, everything just seemed golden. It matched the way she felt inside. Part of her wished she could just live here and not have to deal with any other stuff out there. And maybe she could, but even though she was warming up to the idea of being a soul match to this gentle giant next to her, she couldn't allow herself to be solely dependent on him or anyone here, no matter how nice they had all been to her. She still needed her independence, but maybe she could stay here and just keep working at the diner. That might be enough for her, but first they had to deal with Dale.

Dale. That was a thought she didn't like. Today had been magical, quite literally. Whatever it was that was happening between her, and Abe felt right. The magic she was learning from Bridget made her excited to learn more. Even the dinner with Abe and his brother and Bridget had felt like a family. A family way better than the one she had been born into. All of that made her feel more hopeful than she had ever felt before, but then she would think about Dale and all of that would fade away.

They came up to a clearing. As they came closer to the ledge, she could see for miles. It was beautiful. The sun was just starting to set and there were colorful trees as far as the eye could see.

"Wow, this is breathtaking." She walked closer to the edge to get a better look. Abe slipped in behind her and slid his arms around her waist. Happily, she leaned into him and sighed.

"I hope today wasn't too overwhelming for you," he said softly in her ear.

"No, I really enjoyed it. Bridget taught me so many things. I only hope to remember them. Dinner with all of you was wonderful. And of course... the time when you showed me the spot next to the creek." She turned in his arms and looked up at him. He was looking down at her. The warmth inside of her turned from a shimmering glow to a burning flame. "I think that was my favorite part of the day."

"Mine too."

She reached up on her tiptoes and gave him a quick kiss before turning back in to take in the view.

"So how much of this mountain is the land your family owns?"

"Owns isn't the right word, but almost all you can see. The magic in these mountains is great and I am lucky to be able to live here and keep it safe. Many other mountains have been mined, and the environment and the communities around them stripped of their resources, but we've been able to stop that from happening here."

The sun was setting a little lower and the autumn chill was setting in. Julie shivered in his arms.

"Let's get back to the cabin. I'll get a fire going and get you warmed up," he said, rubbing her arms to warm her up.

"Okay."

He once again took her hand, and they made it back down through the woods on the trail they came in on.

The whole way home, she thought about Abe staying the night with her. She had slept well in his big bed the past two nights, but the thought of waking up in his arms did make her feel warm inside. And as much as she was scared to admit it, the thought of doing things in that bed with him was something she really wanted. This was a new feeling for her, but a welcome one all the same.

They made their way back to the cabin and Abe stopped at the door. "I'll just come in and make you a fire and get everything warm for you," he said.

They walked in and she searched for the courage to ask him to stay.

She watched as he bent down next to the fire. She should just ask him. Just say 'Abe will you stay the night with me', but she couldn't seem to get the words out. He was very respectful, and last he knew she was freaked out about the idea of them being a soul match. But now she was thinking that might be okay. The feelings she had for him were a little overwhelming, but wonderful. She trusted him and that is more than she could say for any man she had known before.

He stood from the fireplace after he got the fire going. The cabin was already filling with a cozy warmth. Their eyes locked. He stood by the fireplace. The air was electric with whatever it was that existed between them.

She didn't have the words, so she just walked over to

him and cupped his face. His beard gently scratched at her fingers as she turned his face towards hers. She licked her lips and caught her bottom lip between her teeth. His eyes stopped at her lips and his breath caught for just a moment as his eyes met hers.

She reached up and kissed him. It was tentative at first. Safe, waiting for the panic. It didn't come, but desire did. She deepened the kiss, and he followed her lead. She took the slight openness of his mouth as an invitation. She licked it with delicious deliberation. His tongue greeted her in an amazing mind-blowing kiss. The magic that existed between them thrummed to life.

CHAPTER TWELVE

Julie

"Abe, will you stay here with me tonight?"

"If it would make you feel safer, I will gladly stay here with you, but just know he can't get you here. He would never be able to find his way."

"It's only partly because of that," she said, trying to be brave. "A part of me that is curious about the relationship between us. Do you really think we are a soul match like she said? Do you feel it?"

"I do feel it, but I won't overwhelm you."

"I'm not feeling overwhelmed by it now. I want to know what you want from me."

"Julie, I want love and companionship, but there's no rush."

"I appreciate that. But I guess what I'm asking is if you had your choice of a life with me, what would it look like?"

"It would look like this, minus the deranged warlock, of

course. I'm a simple man. I belong here on this mountain, but it would be nice to have a companion. Someone to share my life with and my bed with." He shook his head. "I'm sorry Julie, I shouldn't have said that last part."

"I want that too. I want it way more than I should."

His eyes found hers and surprise danced behind them. "You want that?"

She nodded. She wanted it very badly. She had considered such wants shameful for much of her life, but she couldn't help it. The desire for this man was growing inside of her.

She couldn't talk about it anymore, she needed to do it. She needed to experience what she knew he could give her. She could feel safe and lose herself in him knowing he would take care of her. She wasn't sure how she was so certain of that on a deep level, but she'd never been more certain of anything in her life.

She grabbed his face with both of her hands and kissed him. She kissed him with purpose. If he was agreeable, she would have him tonight.

He broke this kiss, which pained her.

"Julie, what is it you want?"

"I want you, Abe. I want a life with you. I can't believe I am saying that because I've only really known you for a couple of days, but in those days my world has been utterly flipped on its head and somehow, I know you're my anchor. I feel that. Do you feel that?"

"I do."

"Will you come to bed with me?" she asked.

He swallowed hard and Julie could see him adjust his pants. "Are you certain?"

"Yes." She took his hand, encouraging him to come with her.

When she looked down, she saw his large erection straining against his pants. It was her turn to swallow hard. He bent down and kissed her, a slow soft kiss. It felt more like the one they had shared on the couch before her life had been turned on its head. But now she was ready for more. She needed more.

She snaked her arms around him, and he did the same. Their mouths connected in this perfect kiss and their bodies pressed into each other. She felt a thrum through her body at the way his erection poked into her belly. She needed more of this man. She needed all of this man. She never knew this feeling was possible.

"Will you come upstairs with me?"

He nodded.

She pulled herself out of this embrace and turned to head toward the stairs. He followed behind her, and she was filled with nervousness. She waited for the panic that didn't come.

"Julie, if at any time you want to stop, just say the word," he said, sensing her pause.

She looked back at him with a warm smile. Those words settled in her soul. She knew them to be true. She knew if she wanted to stop in the middle of the act she was dying to do, he would and he wouldn't begrudge her anything.

"Okay, but can we get a move on," she said with a wink.

At that urging, his earnest eyes turned to hunger, and she felt a pulse between her legs she'd rarely felt before.

When they were both upstairs, she turned to him.

"I'm not super experienced, but I trust you," she said to him.

"As I said, if you want to stop at any time, say the word. It would kill me to know you did anything you didn't want to do. Can you promise me that?"

"I promise." And she meant it.

He sat on the bed and waited for her to join him. She sat down next to him, and he cupped her face and kissed her gently. He had let her take the lead on most of their previous kisses, but this time he was in control. He tested it out. He kissed her slowly and built-up intensity waiting at each step for her to meet him.

He pulled away and laid back on the bed, an open invitation for her to join him and she was more than happy to snuggle up to this bear of a man. She felt safe in his arms, but that wasn't what she was feeling right now. Now, she was filled with desire.

They kissed and their hands explored each other. There were times when he came close to her breasts, but he never went there, and she wanted his hands on her. She needed to let him know she was ready.

She rolled him to his back and climbed on top of him, straddling him. They were both still fully dressed, but that was about to change. She checked in with herself one last time. This was what she wanted. She wanted to be with him in this way. She pulled her shirt off over her head. Her nipples pebbled beneath the pink cotton bra. Her fingers found the buttons of Abe's shirt and she began to undo them.

Once she got them undone, she opened his shirt and looked at him. Hair covered his large chest, and she ran her hands over it. Not even realizing she was doing it, she gently ground her sex against him. He bit his lips and a low rumble sounded somewhere inside of him.

"Can I touch you?" he asked in a low rasp.

"Please."

That was all he needed. His hands that had been resting on her thighs started moving up, over her soft belly and then to her breasts. He touched them with reverence, gently massaging them. She could feel the gentle throb inside of her starting to take over. She reached behind her back and undid the clasp of her bra and then slid the straps down her arms. One swift motion sent the bra across the room and his hands were back to massage her breasts. He propped himself up so he could raise his mouth to them.

He sucked a nipple into his mouth while his hand gently thumbed the other to a peak. She moaned. She wasn't sure where that sound came from, but it seemed to stir something inside of him. He stopped long enough to make sure it was a cry of pleasure. When he was certain it was, he flipped them with ease so that she was on her back, and he was nestled between her legs.

She could feel his cock hard pressing into her through his jeans. She didn't know it could feel like this. He bent down and claimed her mouth while his hand explored her body, her breasts, her belly, her waist. His hand found the button of her jeans, and he paused.

"Is this okay?" he asked.

"Please," was all she could say.

He pressed a gentle kiss to her jaw and neck as he undid the button of her jeans. He pushed them down as she shifted her weight, and he pulled them off. She moved her hand to his jeans; he followed the directive and slipped them off too. Then he was back on her. His mouth was exploring her, her neck, her shoulders, her breasts. He seemed to be everywhere at once and she was getting lost in pleasure. She needed more. He slid his hand down over her belly and further below until his hand was cupping her sex outside of her underwear.

That hand gently squeezed, and she gasped in pleasure. Her whole body was alight with the magic thrumming between them, but she felt another sensation she had never felt before. It was almost like a liquid pooling somewhere deep within her, filling her with pleasure with each stroke of his hand. She needed something, but she didn't know what. She needed a release she had no words to describe.

"Please!" she cried out unsure of what else to say.

He kissed her and slid his hand below her underwear. His fingers slid easily into her sex, and she could hear her wetness as he swirled his fingers around. She might have felt embarrassed, but she was too far gone to care. She had never felt this before. With his other hand, he pulled at the waistband of her underwear, and she shifted her hips as he slipped them down her legs.

Then he slid one finger inside of her to the knuckle then swept up to make tight circles on her clit. The building sensation inside her screamed for release, and she cried out. He slid in another finger in and his thumb found her clit. One circle of his thumb was all it took and the pressure that had been building up inside of her released in waves of pleasure and she cried out. He stayed right there with her his fingers inside of her and his thumb on her clit until the pulsing stopped.

He then pulled his hand back and kissed her sweetly.

"What was that?" she asked.

"If I'm not mistaken, that was an orgasm," he said with a gentle smile.

"Wow," was all she could say.

"Have you never had an orgasm before?" he asked.

"If that's what that was, I have not." she said, still trying to catch her breath.

"That's only the beginning," he said as he bent his head down to kiss her again. "Do you want more?"

"Yes, please, yes," she begged.

He smiled at her with a deep content smile. "Just remember, if I do anything you don't like or want to stop at any time just say the word." His hands were tracing around her body while he said it.

"Yes, I got it." He seemed amused by the slight irritation in her voice. While she liked how respectful he was, she was ready for whatever he had to give her.

His hands continued to learn her body, to worship her body. She had never felt this safe, and this cared for, but also this vulnerable. That should have terrified her, but it didn't. She needed this man, she needed more of this man. His mouth started kissing further down her body. He kissed down her neck and collarbone, she moaned, and he nipped and sucked. He continued to kiss further down until he was kissing right between where her breasts met. One of his hands grasped her breast and his mouth found the other one drawing the nipple into his mouth in a long, slow suck. It felt so good, she could already feel the same feeling building in her again.

His head continued to kiss down her body, down her belly, and over the mound of her lower belly until he was positioned between her legs. And then he did something she didn't expect, he kissed the seam of her sex. No one had ever kissed her there before. She jerked her head up and looked at him. He instantly stopped.

"Is this okay?"

"No one has ever kissed me there before."

"Do you want me to kiss you here?" he asked.

"Yes, I do."

He gave a low grumble that almost sounded like a purr and dipped his head back to her core. He again gave it a gentle kiss. His hand moved to hold her open, and his tongue traced along her until he got to her clit, and he kissed it. He licked up her core again with the flat of his tongue. She gripped the sheets and could feel the need building inside of her again. Then his tongue made soft circles and she cried out, fisting her hands in his hair. He gave a small grunt of approval then he licked her clit again, this time with a little bit more firmness, giving her a little more of what she needed to push her over the edge. She wasn't there yet, but it wouldn't be long.

He pushed a finger inside of her as he continued feasting on her. Then he added another finger inside of her and touched a spot deep inside of her that felt like heaven. Her body convulsed as he swept his fingers over that same spot again. Then he sucked her clit into his mouth and that was it. She broke, her body convulsed, and her voice cried out in pleasure. This time, the waves lasted longer, and he gently fed her pleasure until she was sated.

It was only then when her body lay slack on the bed that she realized how tightly she had his hair fisted in her hands. That was probably painful.

"I'm sorry," she panted.

"What on earth are you sorry for?" he asked with an adoring smile on his face.

"Did I hurt you? I think I pulled your hair."

"You did, but it didn't hurt. It just kept me focused," he said with a wink. "Can I go get you something? A drink?"

"Are we done? You didn't... I mean..." She gestured to his still fully erect cock.

"I think this is enough for now, if that's okay with you. I want you to feel safe and cared for. Maybe we wait on that a little."

"Are you sure? Won't it be painful?"

"What? Not coming? No, not at all."

"Are you sure?"

He kissed her with tenderness she had never experienced.

"Yes, I'm very sure. Are you thirsty?"

She nodded and he winked at her and left to go to the kitchen. Julie sat there. She wasn't sure what had just happened. She thought she knew what was going to happen, but what actually happened was way better than she could have ever dreamed.

Not only did she have her first orgasm, but this man, who had known her for a couple months, and only really known her for a few days had just shown her more love and consideration than anyone had in her entire life. Bridget had said they were soul matches. That thought had terrified her at that moment, but if she got to spend the rest of her life with this sexy gentle giant, she would be happier than she had ever thought she could ever be.

He made it up the stairs with a glass of water. She drank it as he crawled back into bed with her. She laid back down as he slid in behind her. He pulled her close, and they nested together perfectly. She felt good with his big chest pressed tight against her back and his arm around her waist. Letting the feeling of being in his arms wash over her, she drifted off to sleep in his arms feeling completely safe, which might also have been a first for her.

CHAPTER THIRTEEN

Julie

The next morning Julie awoke to Abe's giant body still cradling her, his gentle snores rumbling against her back. She had slept the night in this man's arms, and she had never felt this safe in her entire life. Slowly, she tried to slip out of his hold. He gave a little snuffle and nuzzled right back into her. She felt as if she could stay like this forever, but she did need to pee, and she wanted to make him breakfast.

Take two of getting out of his hold went better. She gently got off the bed and turned to look at him. There he lay, still sound asleep. Although he was human now, she could see the bear inside. After what they did last night, the idea of hibernation with this man seemed to top the list of things she was looking forward to, once the warlock problem was dealt with.

Heading down the stairs, she ran the events of the

previous day in her head. She was a witch. Her family would for sure have kicked her out for that, but she had a feeling the people she was with now were going to become her family.

She found all the ingredients for pancakes and started whipping them up. She was flipping the second batch when she heard him start to wake in the loft upstairs.

"Julie!" he called out, the sleepiness of his voice only slightly covering the edge of panic.

"I'm downstairs making breakfast."

He came down the stairs in a fresh white t-shirt and boxers, his shaggy brown hair rumpled with sleep. He slid behind her, wrapped his arms around her middle, and took a deep breath. His arms tightened slightly as he kissed the top of her head.

"What time do you have to go to work today?"

"Eleven. I'll need a ride unless you think my car is drivable."

"No, I'll give you a ride," he said as he poured himself a cup of coffee.

"What are you going to do while I am at work?" she asked as she plated up some pancakes.

"I'll be at work with you."

"You can't be at work with me. We are supposed to be acting like nothing is different," she protested.

"But there are a couple of things different now," he said and kissed the top of her head. "I'm not going to let him hurt you. I'll be out in the woods. If you see a big bear don't be scared," he said with a wink.

The day went off without a hitch. Julie worked her shift and talked to the regulars. One of the customers did say that he saw a bear in the woods outside. While no one paid him much mind, it did make her smile. Abe came in for dinner and ate with Bridget. Julie wasn't sure how to act around them, so for right now she just treated them like customers, but she wanted to sit down with them and be enveloped in Abe's big arms.

Once the dinner rush was over, Julie clocked out and happily got into Abe's big truck. He was already out in the parking lot with the engine running. She was grateful because the air was cold that night and she didn't have a coat. The warm air from the vent was a relief. She rubbed her hands and put them in front of the vents. Abe watched her with a warm expression on his face. Contentment filled her and she scooted over on the bench seat of the big truck to warm herself right next to him.

"Only one person said they saw a bear today. So do with that what you will," she said with a playful grin. He chuckled and his big hand settled on her thigh. The warmth from it went through her skirt and she moved in a bit closer.

“You look cold,” he said as he started shrugging off his jacket.

“I’m fine.”

He just looked at her with a raised eyebrow and gave her his coat. She wasn’t cold anymore, in fact, she was melting right there in his truck.

The whole way home Julie drank in the warmth and safety of Abe's coat. It is funny how a flannel lined jean jacket could feel like armor. Armor that smelled like pine and earth. Turning her head so the collar rubbed her face she took a deep breath. When she glanced over at Abe, he was watching her with a warm smile on his face. His warm hand found its home on her thigh, and Julie felt an emotion she hadn't had in a long time. Here with this big bear of a man, wearing his oversized coat that smelled like him, she was happy. Even though this was new, even though there was a warlock after her, even though her life had just been flipped on its head, she was happy.

The big truck turned up the well camouflaged road and made its way up the mountain to the little cabin Julie had come to see as home over the past few days. She didn't know it could be like this.

Abe glanced her way and caught her watching him. He gave her a small smile. "What's up?"

"You wanna know something weird?"

"I love weird."

"I'm happy."

The truck pulled up to the cabin and Abe parked. "That doesn't seem so weird to me," he said, sweeping a lock of hair behind her ear.

"Trust me, it's weird," she said with a smile. "I've felt oddly at home since I first set foot on this mountain. I've felt safe with you since I've known you. Those are two things I don't know I've ever truly felt." Her hand reached for his face and the scruff of his beard felt good. It reminded her of where she had felt that scruff last night and thought brought forth another emotion she hadn't felt in a long time either. Desire.

Abe smiled warmly at her and leaned over and gave her a quick kiss before getting out of the truck. He made his way around the truck and opened Julie's door helping her down. He held her hand as he walked her to the door.

"Are you hungry? If you want me to come in, I could make some dinner?"

"Abe, I want you to stay here with me. I like having you around. I like waking up next to you." She reached up on her toes and gave him a kiss.

She turned and unlocked the door. "I do want to take a shower though. I smell like greasy diner food."

"Well, you go shower and I will make some dinner."

They walked into the cabin with a warm familiarity. Julie headed up the stairs to get what she needed for the shower while Abe set to work in the kitchen. Julie got some clothes out of her duffle bag that she still had neatly packed sitting next to Abe's dresser. The idea of putting her clothes into drawers put a smile on her face. It really was the little things.

After she had showered and ate dinner, they were curled up on the couch watching a movie. Julie yawned.

"Why don't you get some sleep? I can head up to my cabin, or sleep on the couch..."

"Abe, I meant what I said. I want you here with me. I want to wake up in your arms again. As crazy as this situation is, you're the best thing to come out of it. You may be the best thing to come into my entire life."

He smiled at her and cupped her face and pressed a sweet kiss to her mouth.

"I feel the same way, Julie. I promise that as soon as the warlock is out of our lives, your happiness will be the top priority of my life."

She leaned over and kissed him. His hand found the small of her back and he pulled her close to him. His lips parted and she slipped her tongue in and clung to his.

"Why don't we go to bed?" he whispered in her ear.

They made their way up the stairs and Abe sat on his big bed. Julie was struck with how much she wanted to do things with this man. Things she had always been taught were shameful. Even in marriage, the things she wanted to do to him were still probably shameful. But when she thought about doing with him, there was no shame. He never made her feel any of those things.

"What's going on in that head of yours?" Abe asked.

"I told you I was raised in a very conservative family. I don't believe what they believe. And after learning what I've learned the past couple days it seems even less true. But it seems like some of those beliefs are just too deep, they are hard to move past."

"What do you mean?" he asked with his deep brown eyes full of patience.

"The things I want to do to you...I was taught that they were only for marriage and even then, it wasn't supposed to be pleasurable, just for procreation."

"There is no shame in anything we are doing," he said, reaching for her hand. "But there's also no hurry." He brought her so she was standing between his legs while he sat on the bed. She knew he meant it. He wouldn't rush her or pressure her, but she was anxious to be with him in that way again. She wanted to bring him even an ounce of the pleasure he had brought to her last night.

"I know. You aren't pressuring me, but I want this." She slipped her sweatshirt up over her head and smiled as she saw Abe's eyes taking in her bare breasts. She wanted the way he made her feel last night, but more than anything, she wanted to make him feel that. She wanted him as lost in pleasure because of her touch as she had been because of his.

She climbed onto his lap, straddling his legs. Her mouth came crashing to his and she was lost in desire undoing the buttons of his flannel shirt. His hands found her ass and pulled her closer to him. The outline of the erection pressing into her thigh shot shivers of desire straight through her.

She gave his shoulders a shove and he fell back on the bed, giving her a victorious smile. She finished unbuttoning his shirt and ran her hand over his large hairy chest and his soft belly. Her fingers ran back up his chest and deliberately rubbed over his nipple and he took in a sharp breath. A small giggle escaped her throat at the effect she had on him.

He cocked his eyebrows playfully and pulled her down to him and rolled them, so he was on top of her. After shrugging out of his shirt, his lips found her neck and continued down to her breast and he drew her nipple into his mouth with a long, slow suck.

At that, her hand found his belt buckle and began fumbling trying to undo it. Abe sat up and undid his belt and laid back down next to her. They both kissed and explored each other's bodies while helping each other out of their pants. She wasn't wearing any underwear underneath her pajama pants, and Abe gave a small whimper as his hands cupped her generous ass. He pressed into her, and she could feel his impressive hardness pressing into her side. She wanted to slide her hands into his boxers which were now the only clothes between them, but when his hand slid between her legs, she lost all thoughts.

She rolled to her back, and he snuggled in next to her and kissed her as his hand explored her. His finger dipped inside of her, then up to that same place he had touched her last night that filled her with so much pleasure, and that pleasure was there again, building with every small circle he rubbed.

She moaned and his lips slanted over hers, swallowing each sound with a deep kiss. He dipped his fingers back inside of her and added another. His tongue moved at the same speed as his fingers. She began to pant, and he broke the kiss and moved his fingers back to her clit and made small circles with a bit more pressure. The pleasure began building inside of her, that feeling she had felt the other night returned. She was just about delirious with pleasure when it broke. Her body convulsed and the pleasure took her over in waves.

She lay there panting and Abe pressed sweet adoring kisses to her chest. She needed to give him the same pleasure. Turning towards him, she reached down into his boxers. He stopped her and kissed her.

"Julie, Are you sure?"

She smiled at him. She loved that he was gentle and patient, but part of her wanted him to feel as out of control as she felt when he did that. She was able to give into it because of how safe she felt around him, now she wanted him to feel that too.

"Please, Abe. I want this. I want to make you feel as good as you have made me feel."

He moved his hand and allowed her to reach into his boxers and wrap her hand around his cock. He was a big man, but even still, the size of it shocked her. She pulled at his boxers, needing to see it. He helped her ease them down over his hips. Then he lay there on his back, his large cock pointing straight up. Julie had never seen anything like it. She stroked it and the way he inhaled and furrowed his brow did something to her. She stroked him again and his hand fisted into the sheets. She was enjoying this. In fact, she wanted to kiss him there just like he had done last night.

She lowered her head and lightly licked the underside of his cock.

"Julie," he rasped out.

"Does this feel good?" she asked as she continued to stroke him.

"So fucking good," he said then bit his bottom lip.

Then she lowered her head and licked him again. She was enjoying this, the feeling that this was shameful and dirty tried to creep in, but the adoring way he was watching her reminded her this was okay. She wanted to make him feel good. Abe deserved to feel good. And to be quite honest, she was enjoying herself just as much. So, she took more of him into her mouth. He hissed and grabbed the sheets. "Fuck, Julie. That feels so good."

That was all she needed. She started working his cock with her hand and sucking him into her mouth finding a rhythm that seemed to work for him. He started panting and she felt so powerful. She took him as deeply into her mouth as she could, and he felt him hit the back of her throat. It made her want to gag, but she couldn't stop. She worked him deeply while her hands worked the part of him that wouldn't fit into her mouth.

His hand fisted into her hair. He didn't guide her movements and continued to let her set the pace. "Julie," he growled out. "I'm going to come."

She pulled off and watched him. As she continued to stroke him at the same speed, her hand easily glided over his slick cock. He grunted and his body tightened as he spurted out over Julie's fingers, chest, and his belly.

"Wow," she said, eyes big looking at them covered in his release.

He reached up and pulled her down for a kiss and she was happy. So happy. He found the flannel shirt he had been wearing and cleaned them both up.

As they both crawled into bed, Julie couldn't help but smile.

"What are you smiling at?" Abe asked as he ran his hands through her hair.

"I can't believe that is something that causes people so much shame. Because I have to say, it feels pretty good to make someone feel something so amazing."

"I'm sorry you've ever been made to feel like what we just did was shameful. It's just part of being a sexual person. As long as both people are fully participating and want it, it can be a beautiful thing."

She sighed contentedly. "My life has been a mess, but whatever has happened, I'm happy to be here with you. Thank you," she said, kissing his chest, not quite able to look him in the eye.

He pulled her chin to meet his gaze. "I'm the one who should thank you. I've been a grumpy bastard, just going through the motions until Bridget brought you knocking on my door. You're what my life has been missing. My life is a better place since you came along."

They looked at each other, holding the vulnerable gaze. She didn't know it could feel like this.

"Ya know, you say this place felt like home almost instantly. Well I have to agree. The moment you set foot in here, it felt like home to me too. It hadn't felt like that for a long time."

She laid on his chest listening to his beautiful words and the beat of his heart. It kept perfect time with hers, like it always seemed to be. His hands continued to run through her hair as her eyes got heavy. Right alongside with the happiness came contentedness as he held her while she drifted off to sleep.

CHAPTER FOURTEEN

Abe

Abe woke up the next morning with Julie still asleep in his arms. He buried his nose in her hair and breathed deeply, smelling honey and almonds. Last night had been amazing, he hadn't expected it, but she was perfect. But he couldn't think about it too much, morning wood was already a problem he was trying to combat before she woke up. But apart from the physical, which he was hoping to reenact again very soon, was the way he had confided in her.

Being vulnerable and sharing parts of himself like he had last night with Julie wasn't how he normally was, but it felt right with her. She was vulnerable in her position through no choice of her own, so he might as well be vulnerable with her as well. She deserved to know what he felt about her. That she had made his house feel like the home it hadn't felt like for years. That he had very deep feelings for her. That when he looked at her, he could see a future with her growing old and gray on this mountain. He just hoped she felt it too, but she seemed to. She kept saying she was scared, but then she kept being brave at every turn. Abe could be brave too.

It had been fifteen years since his parents died and ten years since his sister left, he had shut down when all that happened. But here with her, he saw this mountain becoming home again. That thought filled him with such a deep peace, he would do anything to make that happen, but first, he had a warlock to deal with. Once all that was settled, he was going to do what he needed to do to make Julie happy and stay here with him.

He wanted this mountain to be full of people and love like it had been. That was new considering he had spent the last couple years he spent up here being mad at the world. He didn't feel that way anymore. Ever since she came into his life, his whole view had shifted. His dad always said that is what would happen when he met who he was supposed to be with, but he never knew it would feel this good. He never knew meeting her would change the way he felt about himself and the mountain and the magic in all of it. It had all felt like a burden to him. Being the oldest he was the one who had to stay but it didn't feel like that anymore. It no longer felt like a burden, it felt like a gift. It was not something he had to do, but something he got to do.

He snuggled her in, pulling her close. He only had two thoughts on his mind: getting rid of the warlock and starting his life here with Julie. Okay, well maybe he had another thought on his mind, because he definitely couldn't get that blow job out of his head.

Julie stirred in his arms, he tried to angle himself away so she wouldn't feel his erection pressing into the curves of her glorious ass. He was trying to take things slow with her. He could tell she was carrying around religious trauma from growing up like she did and who knew what else, he would take this at her pace.

She stretched and turned to look at him. He smiled down at her, lightly brushing the hair from her face then pressed a kiss to her forehead. "Good morning," he said in his low rumbly voice.

She smiled up at him with sleepy eyes, "Good morning. I could get used to this." She turned, wrapping his arm around his large chest, and resting her head there.

"Me too," he said moving his arm around her, his fingers lightly tracing her arm.

"So, tonight's the big night."

He nodded. That thought set a boulder in his stomach. He knew that warlock was no match for him and Asher, but with Bridget there he didn't stand a chance. Still, he didn't like the thought of Julie in harm's way for even one moment. "I still don't like it," he grumbled.

"I know," she said, stroking his chest. Then she looked up at him and gave him a little kiss that settled deep inside of him. "But you'll be there and then all of this will be behind us, and we can move on."

Move on? He didn't like the sound of that. "What do you mean move on?"

She looked up at him with a bashful look in her eyes. "Well...ya know, all the stuff Bridget said. We can start a life together...if you still want that of course."

He got lost in the joy of the moment and rolled over her in the bed, caging her below him and he settled in between his legs, forgetting he still had a rather large erection that was now nestled right between Julie's legs. He tried to angle himself away as much as he could, as he kissed her.

"Abe!" she giggled. And that might have just been the best noise he ever heard. "As much as I would love to explore this, I do need to go to the bathroom."

He dropped one more quick kiss on her mouth before rolling off her. "You go to the bathroom. I'll go make us some breakfast."

They both pulled on some clothes and made their way downstairs. While Julie was in the bathroom, Abe started on breakfast. Soon they were both sitting down at the table enjoying a cup of coffee and slow breakfast.

"What time do you have to be down for your shift?" Abe asked.

"I'm on the schedule to come in at four and off at close."

"Okay, so we still have some time. Do you want to do anything today while we wait?"

"I would love to take another walk around the mountain. See if I can see any of the plants Bridget talked about yesterday. I would love to familiarize myself more with the mountain and where they are. I know you probably have work to do, but if you have time, maybe we can do a little bit of what we did last night," she said as she wagged her eyebrows at him.

He couldn't help but laugh.

"I won't be working today. With everything going on, I'm not letting you out of my sight. But I wouldn't say no to any of that," he said, taking hold of her hand over the table. It all felt right, after tonight maybe it could always be this way.

"Why don't we finish up here and we can take a walk?"

Before long they were heading out the door.

"It's chilly this morning," Julie said, hugging her sweatshirt to her.

"Do you have anything warmer to wear?" Abe asked.

Julie just shook her head. He hated that her life had been so neglected she didn't even have a jacket. He opened the door back up and grabbed the jacket she had of his last night and handed it to her. “It's nothing special, but it's yours until we can get one you actually like.”

She slipped it on, and it hung big on her. She rolled up the sleeves, and Abe couldn't help but smile when she turned her head and smelled it with a contented smile on her face. “This is perfect. It still smells like you.”

She took his hand and the magic sparked to life as they set out down the path. He took her back to the stream. If she did plan on staying here and learning more magic, then this is the place she would need to find. His mother had planted all kinds of herbs there she used in her practice. He liked the idea of Julie using them too. He liked the idea of Julie doing just about anything on this mountain.

As they came to the little clearing, Julie let go of his hand and walked over to the stream. "You brought me here again?" she asked with a smile on her face.

“Yeah, I figured there's all kinds of plants here that you might need. This might be somewhere you would want to find easily on your own.”

“It is, thanks.” She looked at some of the plants that were along the edge. “This is mugwort. Did you know that?”

He smiled at her and nodded.

“Bridget says it's good for digestion and trying to conceive.” She picked a leaf and smelled it. “There is so much to learn. I feel like I'm getting a late start. I wish I would have grown up knowing about all of these things.”

“Well, you have plenty of time. Time works a bit differently for us.”

“What are you talking about?”

"Well, if you decide to stay here with me, you might live a little longer."

"I mean I've heard orgasms are good for your health, but that seems like a bit of a stretch," she grinned at him.

He chuckled and shook his head. "Well, as much as I would love to spend all the time in the world exploring that theory with you, I'm referring to some of the mountain magic. People live longer up here."

"Really?"

"Yeah, especially people with their own magic. My grandparents were almost 150 when they died. But I like your theory better," he said, stepping in behind her and wrapping his arms around her as they looked at the stream. "I think we should definitely explore that more."

She turned in his arms and before he knew what had hit him, she reached up and kissed him. He groaned as her tongue swept into his mouth and he knew he was already hard and pressing into her belly. Her hands went to his belt and tried to start undoing it. Covering her hands, he pulled away.

"You don't have to do this."

She looked up at him with a look that just about set him on fire. "Abe, will you stop telling me I don't have to do things? I know I don't have to do things with you, but I want to. I've never explored this part of me, and I am really enjoying myself... and you seem to be too."

"I most certainly am. As long as you don't feel any pressure and are just doing what you want, I'm done stopping you, because I want everything you're willing to give."

"Good," she said as she kissed him and walked him until his back was against a tree. Her hands started to work his belt buckle again and this time he let her. He allowed himself to enjoy the feel of her lips on him. Then she reached into his pants and pulled out his cock and bit her lip. He had never been more turned on in his life.

She held his cock and just looked at it for a moment, like it was something magical. Looking up at him through her eyelashes she began to stroke him. Then she licked the fat head of his cock, and he groaned. He longed to wrap his hand around her hair and buck into her mouth, but this was only the second blow job she had ever given. He would let her figure it out. Even with that, last night had been one of the best blow jobs he had ever had so he was more than happy to let her figure it out with him. But then she sucked him into her mouth, and he hit the back of her throat and her hand cupped his balls and all the thoughts left his head.

"Julie, fuck. That feels so good."

She moaned and the vibration around his cock felt so good, it wasn't going to take long. He clutched the tree behind him trying to hold on to some control. Then she started working the base of his cock with her hands while her mouth worked the rest of him. The longer she worked him, the more control it took to not take control and buck into her mouth. He was teetering on the edge.

"Julie, I'm going to come." But she didn't stop like she did last night. She just kept working him. He tried to gently push her away, but then she grabbed onto his hips and took in deeply into her mouth.

"Fuck," he groaned, as his release overtook him. Julie looked up at him while she swallowed it down. He'd been in love from the moment she stepped into his cabin, but this was something else entirely. He pulled her back up. He needed her right now, on a bed, not in the woods. He shoved his dick back in his pants and buttoned his pants as quickly as he could. Then he picked her up over her shoulder.

She squealed and laughed. "Abe, what are you doing?"

He was already off to the hunting cabin. It was closer than the big one.

"I'm taking you to a bed. Right now."

She just laughed as he carried her to the cabin. When he could see it, he put her down and she grinned up at him with a bigger smile than he had seen before. It made him so happy. He pulled her to the cabin and threw open the door.

It was a small one room cabin. Just a simple bed, small sitting area with a fireplace, kitchenette, and a tiny bathroom.

"What is this place?"

"This is the cabin where I lived when I was building the one we live in now." The fact that he had just said 'we' wasn't lost on either of them. She smiled up at him and his lips came crashing down on hers. He picked her up and walked her over to the bed. Laying her down, he started pulling at her own pants. If he had time, he would have started a fire and have her naked on the bed, but he would settle for this. He could have her like that later, right now he was just overtaken with the need to taste her and bring her pleasure like she just had him.

She fell back on the bed, and he kneeled before her undoing the button of her jeans. She moved her hips allowing him to pull them down. Then she pulled his face to her and kissed him while his hands roamed her body. He squeezed her breast as she sucked his bottom lip into her mouth.

He pulled away looking at her and pushed her knees apart. He moved back to kneel before her and the sight of her spread like this before him lit something inside of him. He ran a finger down her seam. She was so wet. The idea that pleasing him in the woods had made a mess of her did something for him. It woke up the bear inside of him, and he had to taste her right now. He slid a finger in, and he licked her clit.

"Don't ever stop," she said as she fisted her hand in his hair holding his head to her. He didn't intend to stop until she was sobbing in pleasure. He slid in another finger and licked her clit with a bit more firmness. Then she started to grind against his face, and he was hard again. He would never have enough of her. He continued to lick her and work her with his fingers. Her moans grew louder, and he could tell she was getting close.

He sucked her clit into his mouth and her thighs wrapped tightly around his head and he was in heaven. Her body rhythmically pulsed as she cried out and he just kept going. He couldn't stop himself. Breathing was overrated anyway.

Finally, her legs fell open and she pushed his head away. He was still there, kneeling before her. His beard dripped with her release as she lay before him, trying to catch her breath.

He wiped his beard as she propped herself on her elbows and looked up at him. "Abe... that was amazing," she panted at him.

He wasn't a man who needed praise to know his worth, but damn if that didn't fill him with pride.

While Julie cleaned up in the cabin's little bathroom, Abe couldn't help but smile. Both of them had woken worrying about today, but he had taken her mind off of it for the time being. There was a knock at the door. He opened it and found Asher.

"I was wondering where you guys wandered off to," he said. Then he sniffed and cocked his eyebrow giving Abe a knowing look. Being a wolf, he had an impeccable sense of smell and even a human nose could probably have smelled Julie in his beard. “I see you have been busy.”

“What do you want, Asher?” Abe growled.

“Her car is done whenever you want to show her.”

“Asher, what are you doing here?” asked Julie as she came out of the bathroom.

“We have a surprise for you. Come to Abe's when you guys are ready. I’ll meet you guys down there.”

“A surprise!” she smiled at him. Abe found himself jealous of his brother getting a smile like that from Julie, but at least they like each other. It was always better when family liked their partners. That had been part of what had driven his sister away.

“Let's go,” Abe said, reaching out for her hand and the three of them set off. The way she instantly took his hand and wrapped her other arm around him settled that jealousy. She was his and hopefully, would be forever.

When the cabin came into view, Julie's car was sitting there, but it didn't look like her car anymore. It was red and shiny. It looked like a brand-new car.

“Oh my god!” She took off running to the car. “Is this the same car?”

Abe and Asher watched her with almost as much joy on their faces as she had on hers. “What do you think?” asked Asher.

She looked up at them with tears in her eyes. “I can't believe you guys did this!” She ran up and threw her arms around Asher and he hugged her back with his easy smile. Before Abe could feel any jealousy, she threw her arms around him too, and planted a kiss on his lips. Asher tossed her the keys, and she made her way back to the car.

Asher looked over at him with a raised eyebrow and amused grin.

"Shut up," Abe grumbled.

"I'm happy for you man. You got a good one. You get your mate AND we get to catch a warlock. It's been a pretty good month."

Although Abe didn't share Asher's cavalier feelings about the warlock, he did have to agree. It had been a pretty good month, and hopefully after tonight it would be even better.

CHAPTER FIFTEEN

Julie

Later that day, the time came for Julie to go to work. She was busy getting into her uniform and trying to push away the fear that was bubbling up inside of her. Bridget had kept her safe once, and she trusted Abe more than she had ever trusted anyone in her entire life. She looked at herself in the mirror and silently reassured herself that she could do hard things. She headed out to the living room where Abe was pacing.

"I still don't like this. I think I should drive you."

"We have been over this. He has to follow me back. Bridget seems certain he will."

"I know, I still don't like it."

Sliding her arms around his middle, she rested her head on his big chest. He instinctively held her close to him. The magic that thrummed between them was something she longed to explore. Once they got rid of Dale, she might get her chance at a happily ever after, but she wouldn't allow herself to think that yet.

That night her shift went well. Nothing out of the ordinary happened, but about an hour before close, Dale showed up. There were still other people there, and she was grateful for that. She took the trash out to the dumpster while he was inside. She almost had a heart attack when she rounded behind the building and almost ran right into a huge black bear. She screamed and dropped the trash bag.

"You scared me!"

The bear cowered and then gently nosed her hand. Giving his head a pat, she tossed the trash into the dumpster and headed back inside. It was a weird thing to see a bear and not be afraid, but she knew who that bear was, and she was happy he was there, especially with who was inside.

She was happy when Dale paid his check and got in his car and drove away. She finished up all her closing duties and after the last customer cleared out, she was ready to get out of there herself.

She flipped over the open sign and locked up. Her nerves were shot. She felt like everything was about to go wrong. Abe and Bridget had this handled, she reminded herself.

After a deep breath, she headed to her car. The cherry red paint job from Abe and Asher made her smile.

She made her way out of the parking lot and turned onto the highway to make her way to the cabin. She was nervous about finding the turn-off, but Abe had told her she would be able to find it. All the way home, she waited to be followed. Abe and Bridget had both seemed so certain that tonight was the night, but maybe they were wrong because she hadn't seen a single headlight the entire way home. She was glad when she saw the turn-off. She would be back in the safety of her cabin and hopefully in Abe's arms very soon. She wasn't sure how long it would take him to get back, but she knew he would be there soon.

The lights in the cabin were on, he'd left those on for her. She bounded up the stairs and got her keys out of her purse. She went to put the key in the lock, but realized there was something over the lock hole. Upon inspection, it appeared to be a bit of electrical tape. By the time she stopped to examine it, a hand clapped over her mouth and one around her waist dragging her back off the porch.

She tried to scream, but it was futile. He knocked her over the head with something. After the searing pain, everything went black.

When she came to, she tried to stand, only to find her arms were tied uncomfortably tight behind her back. Her feet were bound as well. She had something stuffed in her mouth and duct tape over that.

She opened her eyes, one seemed to be crusted shut. She wagered it was from blood, judging by the searing pain in her head.

She tried to focus on where she was. She was outside, she had no idea how long she had been out. She hoped she was still on the mountain.

She heard Dale talking behind her. She tried to turn to see what he was doing but turning over when you were tied up wasn't all that easy.

"Oh good, you're awake."

A rough hand grabbed her and turned her. She saw she was in a small cave of some kind, and he had built a fire.

"If you promise not to scream, I'll take this off. If you do scream, I'll just knock you out again and put it right back in. Will you behave?"

She nodded. He ripped the tape off her mouth, taking quite a bit of skin with it.

"How'd you find me?" she demanded.

"I put a tracker on your car, an electronic and a magic one. I must say that witch put up quite a few protection spells to try and keep you from me. Maybe after I'm stronger, I can go after that bitch next. Two witches, especially one as powerful as she is, will keep me fed for years."

"How is that possible?" She needed to keep him talking, she knew Abe and Bridget would find her if she could just stall a little bit longer.

"What? You didn't think a warlock like me could get through the magic that little witch and your neanderthal boyfriend put in place?" he spat out. "They don't even know what's coming."

"What are you talking about?"

"You don't even know, do you? You're a dirty little witch. I could smell it on you when you came into the motel. I waited a couple of months because I knew if I could get you on this blue moon, your power would be strong. You left, but I knew where to find you."

He turned away from her and started tending the fire. Julie's eyes darted from the fire to the opening of the cave. Even if she could get out of the restraints, there was no way she could make it past Dale. She needed to keep him talking.

"How did you get past them?"

He turned slowly to her. "Because they underestimated me." He glared at her. "People always underestimate me, but not for long. Our time is coming," he said as he took a dagger from his bag.

Julie's heart started to race. Keep him talking. Abe will come. She kept telling herself that.

"Whose time is coming?"

"The time of the warlock. For centuries, they have been driven out by the witch hunters and the witches. The witches see us as leeches, beneath them, no better than the scum on their shoes. The hunters only sought to destroy all magic. But they've had a change of heart," he said as he examined his dagger. The blade glinted in the firelight. She caught the look in his eyes as his reflected light across his face. He had always looked like a predator, but right now there was a maniacal look in his eye that scared her more. "But the witch hunters and the warlocks have joined forces to take care of their shared problem. Between our magic and their new technology, the tides are about to turn for our kind."

"Technology. What technology?"

"Ahh, dirty witch, I'll only tell you because you won't make it out of this cave alive. The reason I was able to get past the Scottish bitch is because of that. This technology the hunters are creating will change everything. Asher and Abe didn't find me because I was able to hide in plain sight with the cloaking device. Bridget was right inside of the cabin tonight, mere feet from you, but she knew nothing because her old mind can't even fathom what's coming. All I needed to do was knock out the brother and wait for you."

"Knock out the brother?"

"Yes, I knocked him out and tied him up. Then I hid from the witch waiting for you. But I'm all done talking now." He walked closer to her, the big blade clutched in hand.

"What are you going to do with me?"

"I'm going to take your magic. I'm going to slit your throat and drink your blood."

"Abe will find you and he will kill you," Julie spat at him.

"He won't find me. Once we are done here, I'll disappear into the night, and go back to the hunters and the warlocks. Our time is coming. The time of the witch is over."

Before he could do anything, there was a loud roar off in the distance. Her heart soared; she knew that meant Abe couldn't be far behind.

Then, it was as if the forest came to life. The trees were moving as if there were gale-force winds, but no wind blew. There was creaking and crashing of limbs over their heads.

"What the hell?" Dale left the cave to go and see what was happening.

She looked around frantically searching for something to help her cut her bonds.

Before she could find anything, he came running back inside. "Fuck, fuck, fuck. Something's out there?"

"What is it?"

"A fucking bear." He rummaged around in his bag and pulled out a gun. Her heart dropped. He had a gun. She had never heard anything in the planning about what would happen if he had a gun, but she was never supposed to be taken either, so their plan was out the window.

Just then a giant black bear reared up on its hind legs and gave a deafening roar at the opening of the cave. Dale fired one bullet into the beast's body.

"No!" cried Julie, straining against her ties.

The giant bear seemed unphased by the shot and opened its great jaws and clamped them down on Dale's shoulder as he screamed in pain. Julie shut her eyes tight as she heard the bear dragging him out of the cave.

"Stap!" a voice called out in Gaelic. It was a familiar voice. At once everything around her stilled and the bear and Dale and the forest all seemed like someone had just hit the pause button.

A head full of wild red hair appeared at the cave opening. "Well, it looks like this one got away from us," she said as if this were nothing but a little nuisance. "Come, my dear, let's get you back to the cabin."

"Abe was shot!" she called out.

"Aye, he will be alright, but I would really like to get you back into the cabin," she said with more urgency than before.

Julie strained against her restraints.

"Och, goodness me, he really did get a jump on us." Bridget walked over and pulled on the restraints until they fell away. "Now, let's hurry away before the stillness magic wears off."

CHAPTER SIXTEEN

Abe

Abe watched from the woods as Julie got into her car and drove home. Dale's car was still in the parking lot. He watched waiting to see him come out and follow Julie. He needed to follow her there in order to get on the land, he knew that. But he could no longer see Julie's taillights and Dale was still nowhere in sight.

Something was wrong.

Something had gone wrong; he could feel it. He never liked this plan. He needed to get to her right now. He needed to find Julie and check in with Asher and Bridget.

When he crossed the magic line and he could sense Julie, they were already connected. She was in trouble. He headed for the cabin to see if he could pick up her trail, but he didn't make it that far, on the way he picked up her scent. There she was, her honey and almond Julie smell, but now it was intermixed with blood. He roared and took off running in the direction.

With that roar, the mountain woke up. He still had no clue how this could have happened. The magic on the mountain should have already been alerted to a warlock, but it hadn't been. But once Abe woke it up the magic began pulsing through the trees. It would help Julie. She would be okay. She had to be okay.

The trail led him to a cave. It was a cave he knew well, being a bear, he knew most of the bear sized hidey-holes on this mountain. As he came closer, he could hear Dale talking. When he heard Julie answer back, his heart nearly leapt out of his chest. While he was relieved to know Julie was alive, she was still in danger, and he needed to get to her.

Dale emerged from the cave to check things out when he turned and saw him in the shadows. Dale ran quickly back into the cave, but Abe was on his tail.

“It's a fucking bear!” Was all Abe heard as he stood on his hind legs and roared into the cave. Then she watched as Dale pulled out a gun and fired it. Abe's teeth clamped down on his shoulder and began to pull him into the woods. He would deal with this warlock now.

He pulled him further into the woods. Asher had caught up with him and ran alongside him. Once they were up the mountain, Abe threw Dale to the forest floor and put a heavy paw on his chest and roared in his face. His face was lit up in terror.

As that was happening, the mountain started to claim him. Vines wrapped around his arms and legs. Abe finally took his paw off as the vines wrapped around his chest. Dale gave out a final cry and the vines took him, and the forest claimed him. Abe roared once more, and Asher howled next to him.

The warlock was dealt with. He wouldn't be hurting her anymore, he was no longer a threat, but none of that would matter if Julie wasn't ok. Abe took off towards the cabin. He became more and more aware of the gunshot wound, but the adrenalin still coursing through his body got him to the cabin.

When they got closer both men shifted back. Once back in his human body, Abe collapsed. The wound made it hard for him to keep moving. Asher got him to his feet, shouldering his weight he guided him up the stairs.

The light was on, and he could see Bridget in the kitchen. The two came crashing through the front door.

"Bridget!" Asher frantically called out.

CHAPTER SEVENTEEN

Julie

They weren't too far from the cabin, but by the time they made it back safely, the forest had woken. The trees were moving and swaying. Dale's screams and the roar of a mighty bear were all that was heard over the trees.

Once they were at the cabin, Bridget picked up the keys that lay discarded on the porch and unlocked the door and got them both inside.

"Is he okay?" Julie demanded.

Bridget held her face with both of her little hands. "He is fine. I promise you that. You are safe. The forest is claiming the warlock as we speak, I imagine your bear will –"

At that moment the door came crashing open. Julie screamed.

"Bridget!"

Julie watched in horror as these men stood in the doorway naked and bleeding. Asher was helping Abe to stand.

"Bring him in." Bridget moved a chair away from the table for Abe.

He reached for Julie, she came instantly to him and fell to her knees before him.

"Abe!" Her eyes scanned him in horror.

"I'm okay. Are you okay?"

He brought her to his chest in a tight bear hug, she winced a little, because while she was safe, she was in quite a bit of pain. He pulled back and looked at her. She raised her hand to her head and pulled it back bloody. Her hands started to shake, and she suddenly felt cold. He brought her in for another gentler hug that helped, though she still shook.

"Bridget, I think she is going into shock," he said, his voice filled with panic.

"Of course, she is," she answered back, not panicked in the slightest. "Asher, are you feeling well?"

"He caught me by surprise when I was still at the barn. He knocked me out and tied me up." He rubbed his head and took a breath. "I'm fine. I'm just not sure how all this happened. He shouldn't have gotten by me like that."

"Nonsense, Asher. Don't feel bad for a moment. He got the jump on all of us, but we finished the job." She set down cups of tea in front of them. "Drink this, drink it all. It has my strongest healing medicine for your wounds, and it will help with the shock."

Julie sipped the tea; it tasted like orange and cinnamon. It was the most delicious tea she had ever tasted. With each sip, she felt the panic leave. She looked at her wrists where her arms had been bound and the bruises were gone, the tender flesh around her mouth where the duct tape had been ripped off was no longer painful. She raised her hand to her head and only felt the sticky blood crusted over her hair. The wound was gone, and the pain had stopped. She finished drinking the tea and felt good as new.

"How are you feeling now, my dear?" she asked with a warm smile.

"Much better. How are you? You were shot!" she said to Abe.

"I was ok, but now I'm even better," he said looking at the tea in his cup. "This is quite the magical remedy."

"Right?" said Asher, rubbing his head. "I feel fine now."

"Aye, ye can thank the fae for that one, though I don't think they would much approve of me using that magic to heal humans, but when have they ever approved of me?"

"Are you okay?" she asked Abe again.

"Yes, I'm okay. I'm so sorry we failed you. I blame myself. I should've checked the car for a tracker when we were repairing it."

"How could you have known? What happened to Dale?"

"He's gone," he said plainly.

"What do you mean? Did you kill him?" she asked.

"No, I wanted to, but I dragged him out into the mountains, and it took him."

"Took him where?"

"Some questions of such ancient magic are better left unanswered, but he'll never bother you again."

She fell into his arms, and he held her. The dampness of his skin made her pull back. He was covered in blood and naked.

"I'm fine now, as I assume you are. It pays to have a white witch with the power of the fae on your side." He smiled over at Bridget who just held up her teacup with a smile and a twinkle in her eye.

"The only mystery left is how on earth he got past us?" Bridget seemed perplexed. Normally Bridget was all knowing, but right now she looked just as confused as all of them.

"When we were in the cave, he was talking about witch hunters," Julie said, trying to remember what else he had said. It was all jumbled in her head.

"Witch hunters?" Bridget asked her with a shocked look on her face.

"Yeah, something about the warlocks and the witch hunters coming together," Julie said, trying to remember what he had talked about.

Asher, Abe and Bridget all shared a questioning look and waited for Julie to continue.

"There was something about the magic of the warlocks and the technology of the witch hunters. He was able to hide because of their cloaking tech and find his way here because of the trackers he put on my car."

"That would explain things," Abe said with a concerned look on his face.

"Nothing good can come of those two teaming up," said Asher.

"Do you think this will happen again?" asked Julie.

"Not with Dale," she said with a kind smile. "But with the unholy joining of the hunters and the warlocks, I fear this is just the beginning," Bridget said, her eyes catching Abe's.

"But now that we know, we can be prepared," Abe said, cupping Julie's face. "You're safe here. Tomorrow, Asher and I will make sure the mountain is still protected. We know what magic to put in place, and we will know to look for more technology this time."

"Technology..." Bridget grunted. "It's changing everything about the old ways."

"We'll figure it out," Abe said in a reassuring tone. "But there is nothing left to be done tonight. Let's just get some sleep."

"Well, I think I'll leave you two to it." She set her cup in the sink and headed for the door. "I'll be around sometime tomorrow to check on the both of you. Asher, will you walk me to my cabin?"

He opened the door and the two of them left and Abe locked the door behind them.

CHAPTER EIGHTEEN

Julie

"Why don't you go get cleaned up? I think we both need a shower."

She knew she needed a shower. She needed to wash away all the crusted blood, but she wasn't ready to be apart from him. The idea of him being out of arm's reach wasn't something she could bear.

"Will you come with me?" she asked tentatively, looking down in her teacup.

He put his big warm hand over hers and waited until she looked up at him. "Yes."

Once in the bathroom, Julie stopped to look in the mirror while Abe got the water going. She examined herself, all the bruises and everything were gone. All that was left to show there was any near-death experience was the blood that caked her hair to her face and covered her shoulder and back. Abe stepped into view in the mirror behind her and gave her a soft smile. He was already naked. While the wound was gone, his abdomen was still covered in blood.

"So, you're a big black bear, huh?"

He nodded. "Does that scare you?"

"Not even a little." She reached up on her toes and kissed him. His fingers began to work at the buttons of her uniform dress from the diner. "I think I'm going to need a new uniform." This one was crusted with blood and dirt and ripped in a few different places.

"Do you? You could just live up here with me. I'll provide everything you need."

He looked at her in a way that promised a happy ending, but she wasn't sure she wanted that. She wanted a happy ending for sure, but she didn't want to stop working at the diner.

"I appreciate that, I do, but I need my own money. Not because I don't trust you, just for my own peace of mind."

He nodded and smiled at her, "Of course, whatever you want, but maybe you can take a few days off. I'm not sure I'm ready to let you go just yet."

"That I can do."

He bent his head and kissed her. All those butterflies she felt around him came back to life, and the magic danced between them. She could use a couple of days off to spend with this wonderful man. The warm water ran over her, rinsing away the blood and dirt. She washed away the blood coating his abdomen where he'd been shot and found nothing underneath it but perfect skin, not even a scratch. He helped wash away the blood and mud from her hair. As the water started to run clean, he bumped into her, jabbing his fully erect cock into her belly.

"Sorry, that thing has a mind of its own."

"Well, I happen to like where his mind is at right now."

She reached up and grabbed his face and brought it down to hers. She kissed him with all the passion she felt. She'd never had a man who cared for her the way he did, who had shown her as much love and compassion as he had in these few days. She loved him and as she thought those words, she waited for the panic that didn't come. Hope came in its place; she was hopeful for what a life with him would be like and that felt amazing.

"I have to tell you something," she said tentatively.

"Anything."

"I think I'm falling in love with you."

"I've been in love with you since I first saw you. I'm glad you're finally catching up."

She smiled and playfully poked him in the ribs. He took her hand and pressed a gentle kiss to it. "Let's get dried off and get to bed, if you're up for it."

"Not only am I up for it, but I'm really hoping you'll finally make love to me tonight, because that's what this is. It is love, and I want to feel that."

Stepping out of the shower, Abe took extra care drying her off. Even though there wasn't a scratch or an ounce of pain from the attack, he still treated her with tender care. Bridget's tea had healed her physically, but Abe's love healed her emotionally. He was the first person she had ever trusted like this, let alone the first man. If he was agreeable tonight, she wanted all of him. She hadn't yearned for a man like this before.

Once they were both dry, they headed up to the bedroom. She was starting to feel a little nervous.

"Just so you know, I'm not super experienced," she said. She bit her lip and looked at the rug on the floor. She toed the tassels on the edge waiting for the boldness she felt in the shower to return.

"I'm not all that experienced myself, but I know what exists between us is special, the act of physically bonding will be very powerful." He gently lifted her chin, so she was looking at him. "I want you to feel at ease, this is entirely your decision. I very much want anything you are willing to give me, but I can be patient if that is what you need. I'm not going anywhere."

Those words were all she needed. The nerves that lingered turned from apprehension to excitement. She wanted this man, and she wanted him more than she could ever remember wanting anything. She reached up on her toes and threw her arms around his neck and kissed him. The suddenness of her move threw him off balance and they toppled onto the bed.

He chuckled, but then he kissed her. He kissed her deeply and then kissed down her jaw and neck. His hands were all over her, her breasts, her waist, her hips, her belly. She was alight with the sensation of his touch. He kissed down her belly and his hand found her sex. First, he just squeezed, and she ground into his hand.

He slipped a finger between her folds and spread her wetness over her aching center. She needed his man. She needed to be filled by him. He slid in one finger, then two, and he started working her slowly. Then his tongue flitted over her clit. She was going to come so quickly. She was ready for this man to claim her. She had never wanted to be anyone's before, but she knew belonging to this man would mean safety and contentment. He sucked her clit into his mouth, and she fell apart.

When she was done, he sat kneeling between her legs.

"Do you still want to do this?" he asked.

"Yes!" she cried out enthusiastically.

She needed him right now. He needed to be inside of her, filling her. She reached up and pulled his face down to hers and kissed him. The taste of herself on his lips only fueled the fire inside of her. He reached for a condom from the bedside table and smoothed it over his cock.

He smiled. God, she was ravenous for this man. She gasped as he gently pushed into her. He slowed and checked in with her. She looked up into his warm eyes. His pupils were blown with desire as he slowly pushed all the way in. Once he was fully sheathed inside of her, he ground in, rubbing against her clit. She clung to his big back, digging her nails in. In that moment, she was so full of pleasure and so full of him, she didn't think she was existing in the same reality anymore.

The magic that danced between them came crashing through. He began to pump in and out of her. She felt as if her earth was spinning off its axis in the best possible way. She wrapped her legs around his waist in an attempt to hold onto him and this feeling. He bent his head and kissed her. Once they were connected in so many ways, it was as if the feeling of spinning out of control stopped, and she was anchored to him. The world was spinning around them, they were at its center. The magic swirled around them like a gentle tornado blowing around them and caressing them.

She clung tightly to his body as he continued to thrust in and out of her. She could feel her release building inside of her. She was going to come again. "Abe," she gasped out. Then the waves of pleasure started hitting her in the most intense orgasm she had ever experienced. The wind and magic swirled around them as wave after wave of pleasure broke over her body.

A deafening roar came from his mouth and slammed

into her one last time, he pulsed inside of her as the waves of pleasure took them both and the magic swirled around them, but they were firmly anchored to each other.

He collapsed onto her, propping himself up on one elbow, as they caught their breath. He kissed her sweetly and then pulled out of her and fell to her side. She reached for him, and he gathered her into his arms. She rested her head on his chest, listening to his heart thunder inside his chest.

"What was that? I've never felt like that before?" she asked, still trying to catch her breath.

"Me either," he answered back. "I'm beginning to think Bridget knows what she's talking about when she says soul matches, because that was incredible. I could feel your magic."

"I could feel yours too, and it would seem my magic is as smitten with you as I am."

"I'm not sure how it all works, but I'd be willing to spend the rest of my life finding out."

He froze. He was afraid that what he had just admitted might scare her, but she was never going to run from this man or this place. She wasn't sure she would be capable of leaving him; besides she desperately wanted a life with him. She wanted to spend her days with him and her nights doing this with him, over and over. This was a new feeling but a welcomed one.

"I want that too," she said.

"You do?"

"I really do. I meant what I said downstairs, I love you. I'm not sure what the future looks like, but I'd be pretty okay if it looked just like this."

CHAPTER NINETEEN

Julie

Julie woke up the next morning, it would be easy to believe that yesterday had been a dream, except her proof was holding her tightly and snoring gently. She took a deep breath, one that hadn't come that easy in a long time. Last night had been a nightmare, she had been bashed over the head and kidnapped by a warlock, her boyfriend had been shot trying to save her, they both made it out okay and the warlock is gone. That is a night for the books as far as anyone was concerned.

But what else happened that night was like nothing she had ever dreamed of. While Julie wasn't a virgin, what had happened with Abe last night was what she would consider to be the first time she made love. And what happened between them when their magic connected was like nothing she could have even dreamed of. It was like a tornado of love and magic.

She tried to turn to look at Abe, but he was holding her tightly. He had been so scared last night. What he had feared had indeed happened, but it all turned out okay in the end. She couldn't help but smile at how tightly he was holding her. It would be annoying later, but right now it felt good to be held close to this big, beautiful man. The idea that they could live a quiet life together on this mountain filled her with a deep sense of peace.

She moved in his arms again and he stirred away. “Good morning, little witch,” he grumbled in her ear.

“Good morning, my love,” she said as he rolled in his arms to face him. She cupped his face and kissed him and let her fingers scratch a little in his beard. “Last night was pretty wild, huh?”

“Which part?” he asked rolling onto his back and Julie draped herself across him.

“I mean, take your pick.”

“Well, if I get to pick it is going to be the part that happened here in this room. I'm hoping for a repeat of that soon,” he said as he kissed her again.

“I think I am going to call Betty and tell her I'm not going to make it in today,” she said.

“Good, I don't want you out of arm's reach all day. You’re mine and I'm gonna need you close by.”

“I'm not going anywhere. And I’m more than happy to spend the day close to you. Hell, we could even spend the day together in this bed,” she said, giving him a big grin. But as soon as she said that her stomach growled.

“I think my little witch might need some breakfast first,” Abe said as he kissed her forehead. "Let's go see what we can find."

They both got out of bed and started to pull on clothes. Julie stopped Abe and examined where he had been shot yesterday. It was perfectly healed, with no evidence of the night before.

"I'm good. Are you feeling good?" he asked, brushing hair behind her ear.

"Yeah, I'm fine. It's so weird. I mean, I'm glad we are both physically fine, but it does make the whole thing seem like a nightmare."

"Well, it was a nightmare."

"You know what I mean, it feels like it never happened."

"It definitely happened, but I'm so glad you're safe now." He pulled on his t-shirt as Julie dug through her duffle bag for a clean t-shirt. "I cleaned out the top drawer of the dresser for you. I'll make you your own dresser and we'll figure out where everything goes. I want you to be at home here, Julie. If you're still wanting to be here after everything last night."

"Oh Abe, you silly old bear. I'm here for good. I'll unpack after breakfast."

He swept her up in a big hug holding her up off the ground and planted a big kiss in her lips. She couldn't help the giggle that escaped her lips.

"Let's go make some breakfast."

They went down and started breakfast. Before long, there was a knock at the door and Asher and Bridget walked in.

"Pancakes?" asked Julie.

"I knew you'd be nice to have around," Asher remarked with a big grin as he sat down at the table.

"That sounds delicious, dear. Thank you." Bridget said joining Asher at the table.

Julie smiled as she doubled the pancake recipe and started cooking. Abe frowned at the company. "Didn't we get enough togetherness last night?"

"Don't worry, Asher and I won't be in your hair long. I just wanted to ask if I could stay at one of the cabins up here for a while. Now that Dale is taken care of, I would prefer not to stay at the motel a moment longer."

"Of course," Abe said. "You can have one of the hunting cabins, or Esther's house is open. It's a bit bigger."

"Funny you should mention Esther," Asher said carefully.

The energy in the room shifted. Julie was taking the first batch of pancakes off the griddle, and she looked over to see Abe glaring at Asher.

"What are you talking about?" Abe asked.

"Now, it's all going to be okay. I plan on staying for a little while longer," Bridget said, putting her hand on Abe's chest.

"Asher..." Abe said as a warning.

"Esther's back," said Asher.

"Is she alone?" Abe asked.

"It is just her and Ruby."

Abe took a breath. "Good. I'm glad she is back. How is she?"

"I haven't talked to her yet. I saw her unpacking on my way over."

As much as Julie wanted a day of nothing in bed with Abe it looked like it was going to have to wait, but she was interested in meeting his sister.

"Well, let's eat," Abe said. "We'll let them settle in and invite them over for dinner. Bridget, you can stay here as long as you want. You know you are always welcome."

Julie was taking the next batch of pancakes off when Abe came over and slipped in behind her, wrapping his arms around her. She gave a contented sigh and settled into him. Asher and Bridget were talking about last night and getting what cabin she would be in decided. Abe was behind her. Things felt right, and to imagine a week ago she was alone in a dingy motel room dodging the advances of Dale.

She never would have dreamed this is where she would end up. A witch in love with a bear shifter and getting her own little magical family. Life was pretty perfect. She took off the final batch of pancakes and carried them over to the table and Abe brought the syrup behind her. Together, the four of them sat down and had breakfast all feeling a bit lighter with the warlock being gone and everyone now knowing and accepting their place.

Asher and Bridget left to get her settled in one of the cabins, leaving Julie and Abe alone.

"How are you feeling about your sister being back in town?" Julie asked.

"Good, I think. We'll have to find out what brought her back, but it will be good to see her and her daughter. We'll hopefully meet them tonight," he said as he was walking closer to her.

Once he got to her, he rested his hands on her hips. "But right now, I don't really want to talk about my family," he said with a look in his eye that shot right to her core turning her molten.

"Oh really? What would you like to talk about?" she asked with feigned innocence.

"No more talking, let's do an experiment," he said in a low, gravelly voice.

"An experiment? How scientific," she answered back with a smile.

"Let's see if your magic reacts to mine the same way it did last night," he said, sweeping her off her feet and carrying her over to the steps. "As much as I want to carry you up these steps, they're a little steep, so I'm going to put you down," he whispered in her ear. "But then you are going to go straight up there, and we are going to get undressed and perform our experiment."

She turned to him and kissed him deeply, putting everything she could into the kiss.

"I am very much looking forward to it."

They both made their way up the stairs and made love again, and while it wasn't quite as earth shattering as it had been last time, it was still just as magical. But this time instead of the magic being an outside force it was something she felt deep inside. It was love, the magic of the love she felt for this gentle giant was magical in its own right and she was excited to see how their life would play out.

EPILOGUE

Julie

2 years later

Sometimes Julie couldn't believe she had been living here on this mountain for two years. She never imagined anything like this would be possible for her. She had been on her own, struggling for almost a decade until this little old Scottish witch showed up at the diner one day and changed everything.

Now she was surrounded by family and friends, and life was good. When she and Abe got together, she didn't think she would ever want kids because everything she had gone through made her a bit apprehensive. But once she got on this mountain, she was beginning to see the world differently.

Abe had changed everything for her. He was patient and kind. While he was still a grumpy ol' coot sometimes, as

Bridget liked to call him, he was never cruel and endlessly doted on Julie.

In her time on the mountain, she'd seen the way he showed up for his family, the way he took care of his niece, and she fell a little bit more in love with him every day.

Abe still ran the woodworking business with his brother. Julie worked part-time at the diner, but people had also started to come to her for healing magic and even some love spells. While she was nowhere near as good as Bridget, she did enjoy helping people. It was a good life, but it was about to change, and she couldn't wait to tell Abe.

While he had been working, she made a special dinner for him. He had come home and gotten in the shower, and she had set it all up.

"What's this?" he asked coming out of the bathroom as Julie finished lighting the last candle at the table.

"I have something I wanted to talk to you about," she said with a smile.

"You made lasagna? It must be good news," he said sitting down across from her.

"I hope so," she said, watching him take the first bite.

"This is delicious," he said, reaching over and taking her hand across the table. "What's the news?"

"I wanted to talk to you about the addition we have been talking about adding to the back of the cabin," she said with a smile.

"Okay, we can talk about that," he said with a confused look on his face.

"How long do you think it would take to build?" she asked.

"If I can get Asher and I on it, I don't think it would take too long," he said, eyeing her suspiciously.

"Like maybe you could finish it in nine months?" she asked, grinning at him.

"No!" he gasped.

"Yes! I found out this morning."

He stood from the table, his chair clattering down loudly on the floor behind him. He walked around the table in a few big strides and pulled Julie up from the chair and into his arms. He spun around and she giggled in his ear.

"We haven't even been trying that long. Are you sure?"

She just nodded and smiled. His lips came crashing down on her and he made his way to the stairs. Dinner would have to wait. They had some celebrating to do first.

While her life wasn't perfect, it was better than anything she could have dreamed. She was deliriously happy and hopelessly in love, nothing else really mattered after that.

SPOTIFY PLAYLIST

Magic in the Mountains Playlist

Take Me Home, Country Roads - Brandi Carlile
Twin Peaks Theme - Angelo Badalamenti
Labour - Paris Poloma
Hibernate With Me - Benjamin Scheuer
Feels Like Home - Chantal Kreviakzuk
When You Say Nothing At All - Alison Krauss & Union Station
Extraordinary Magic - Ben Rector
Savage Daughter - Sarah Hester Ross
I Am Yours - Andy Grammar
How Sweet It Is (To Be Loved By You) - Amber Leigh Irish
One Day At A Time - Jeremy Voltz
Have You Ever - Brandi Carlile
Wildflowers - The Wailin' Jennys
I Like To Be With With Me When I'm With You - Drew Holcomb & The Neighbors
Grow Old With You - ortoPilot

SPOTIFY PLAYLIST

Season Of The Witch - Lana Del Ray
How Long Will I Love You - Ellie Goulding
Better Place - Rachel Platten

Also by Mary Warren

A Highlander for Hannah *Mystic Falls 1*

Spotlight on Poppy *Mystic Falls 2*

Lexi Lets Go *Mystic Falls 3*

The Bargain

Coming Soon! Winter 2024

Reclaiming Kate

Mystic Falls 4

Stay up to date with all the up and coming books and everything else Fat Girls in Fiction related with my *NEWSLETTER*

ACKNOWLEDGMENTS

So much goes into writing a book. This one started at a story in an anthology called I am the Fire. All of the money raised from that anthology went to the national abortion fund. I am proud to have been a part of that anthology and the important cause we supported.

As always I have to thank my amazing partner. I could not do any of this without him. He is my support and my sounding board.

Also my editor Lexi at Morally Grey Edits. She helps me to tell the best stories possible and I love working with her.

And with this book I was able to work with a new cover designer. Rowan Merrick is a dream and I love what she did with Abe and Julie. (Also did you see that honey bottle she's holding and Abe's bear shadow... I just love it!!)

And as always I am thankful to be a part of the wonderful bookish community. I find so much joy and support in all of you. From the veteran authors showing me the ropes to the new authors who are turning to me for advice... I don't have much yet, but I'm learning.

And thank you! I could not do this without my readers. I am so grateful for everyone who has taken a chance on Abe and Julie, and all the other couples. I hope you stick around and see what Bridget has up her sleeve next.

ABOUT THE AUTHOR

Mary Warren lives in Illinois with her family. When she's not writing stories of fat women, she's reading them and advocating for better fat representation. Mary founded Fat Girls in Fiction, pointing out positive fat representation for women, femmes, and non-binary people in books. This project became a community and is something she is immensely proud of and happy to be working on.

Printed in Great Britain
by Amazon

52811468R00098